ʒ ⁻ ⁻ ⁻ ⁻
number on the

Ace High in Wilderness

It has been seven years since the Civil War ended. Ex-sharp-shooter John Wright has tried to forget the horrors of his incarceration in the Confederate POW camp at Andersonville, where he watched, powerless, as one of the guards murdered his childhood friend.

Now, two ex-prisoners show up, telling John they have tracked down the murderous prison guard and need help bringing him in. They offer John a share of the reward. But all is not as it seems and John is about to find out that the road to justice is rocky indeed. . . .

By the same author

Rangeland Justice
Hope's Last Chance

Ace High in Wilderness

Rob Hill

A Black Horse Western

ROBERT HALE · LONDON

ISBN 978-0-7090-9067-0

Robert Hale Limited
Clerkenwell House
Clerkenwell Green
London EC1R 0HT

www.halebooks.com

For Val and Joss

Typeset by
Derek Doyle & Associates, Shaw Heath
Printed and bound in Great Britain by
CPI Antony Rowe, Chippenham and Eastbourne

PROLOGUE

Fort Sumpter Prisoner of War Camp,
Andersonville, Georgia 1864

John knew he was drowning. The faces above him were blurred and the sounds were far away. He could make out voices. There was some disturbance. But it was comfortable under the water. Tiredness flowed out of his limbs; it was warm; he did not feel hungry any more. Then someone reached down and hauled him out of the water by his throat. He was choking, gasping. As the water fell off him he knew it was not water, it was empty air. His clothes were dry. It was dark. Someone was kneeling on his chest holding a knife at his throat. He was shocked to realize he had been dreaming not drowning.

'Which one wuz it?'

The voice was a heavy Alabama drawl. 'The young one.'

'I can't see a damn thing. Which one's that?'

John felt the blade nick his neck as he turned towards where his friend Billy had been asleep beside him. Another man was kneeling on him. John could just make out his silhouette. He was holding a long Confederate bayonet at Billy's throat.

5

'Hand over that watch. The one I seed yuh usin' today. Which one o' you Yankee boys got it now?'

He waited for an answer.

'Come on, you're in Georgia now. If you wake up in the mornin' with yer throats cut, it won't make no difference to nobody.'

John felt the man kneeling on him go through his pockets with one hand, while keeping the blade pressed against his windpipe with the other.

Then the place erupted. Billy gave a yell and was fighting the man sitting on him. The tussle lasted for a full, violent minute. The whole, frail shebang shook. John kicked out, trying to rid himself of the man planted on his chest. Then he heard Billy groan. He saw the guard slide his bayonet up under Billy's rib cage. The fighting stopped like a sudden change in the wind.

'You get it?'

'Yeah.' The guard's voice was as dry as sand.

'Now, you listenin'?' John felt the guard kick him in the leg. 'We're gonna go now. When he takes that knife away, don't you go jumpin' up now. You just lie there quiet till we're gone. Else I'm gonna have to stick you in the guts as well.'

The guard who had taken the watch from Billy lifted the canvas door. He was silhouetted against the grey dawn light, the bloody bayonet in his right hand, a gun in his left. The other guard slowly moved the blade away from John's neck and began to get to his feet.

As soon as the crushing weight was off him, John shoved the man aside. Together, they toppled the main pole and the whole tent came down. A gun went off. The men thrashed around trying to free themselves from the sea of canvas. The guards broke free. One of them smashed his boot heel into John's face, as he shoved his way out into the open. John threw himself after him.

Outside, John saw the men dodging through the lines of prisoners' tents up ahead. One of them was calling out to the guards in the pigeon coops on the perimeter fence. John launched himself at the second man and brought him crashing down on top of a group of prisoners sleeping out in the open. The man stumbled to his feet, treading on the prisoners lying on the ground. John grabbed hold of the guard's coat with his left hand and held on. The guard slashed at John's fingers with his bayonet.

Pain seared John's hand like a branding iron. The guard pulled away. John collapsed on to the ground, clutching his injured hand, now slippery with blood. The guards in the pigeon coops where shouting now and training their rifles on the prisoners. Someone grabbed hold of John and lay on top of him. Other prisoners moved in close to hide him from the guards.

After a while, the guards in the turrets lost interest. There were disturbances like this fifty times a day. It was safe now. The prisoners moved away from John. The one who had lain on top of him was a thin, dirty-faced man of about thirty. He grinned at John through chipped teeth. John was faint from his wound. He uncovered his hand slowly: there were two fingers missing.

One of the prisoners tore a strip off his shirt and bandaged John's hand tight. John lay back as the pain pulsed through him.

'They killed my friend,' John said. 'Came in the night an' stole his watch. Killed 'im because he wouldn't let 'em take it.'

'Them's Johnny Rebs,' one of the prisoners said. 'They'd steal your wife an' eat your children, I reckon.'

'We gotta get outa here,' John said.

'You jus' lie back, now. You jus' worry about takin' care of that hand. . . .' He paused. 'New York boy, ain'tcha?'

'John Wright from Brooklyn. First Battalion Sharp-shooters.'

'I'm Mikey Donnal from Five Points, Second Infantry. You just rest awhile, John Wright,' Mikey said. 'I'll send me cousin Sean off to find us some food. They should be handin' out a ration o' beans an' weevils shortly. Sean complains about the weevils, but I keep tellin' him weevils is meat. The only thing wrong with 'em is that they ain't fat enough. We can't be choosin' not to eat 'em now, can we?' Mikey grinned. 'That would be plain ungrateful.'

That evening, John went back to where his shebang had been. Billy's body was covered with a torn army-issue jacket. Someone had taken the canvas covering and the wooden supports. The bowls and spoons were gone too. A thin, malnourished prisoner lay on the ground close by. His ragged uniform was too big for him. His eyes bolted out of his head. He spoke softly.

'Didn't want to call the dead cart till you'd been back,' he said. 'I covered 'im up. Some fellas from the Pennsylvania Cavalry took the canvas. I couldn't argue with 'em. I didn't know where you was.'

'That's all right,' John said. 'I seen 'im now. You can call the dead cart.'

Grief twisted inside John like a blade. He had known Billy all his life. They had grown up on the same street. The Brooklyn waterfront had been their playground. Memories of their childhood games tumbled in front of his eyes: swimming in the East River, running through the crowds in State Street Market, playing baseball in Prospect Park, fighting the kids from Flatbush. Later, they were thrilled when the war came and brought with it a promise of adventure.

Full of hope, Billy and John had enlisted together, but their adventure was short-lived. They survived the horrors of Yorktown and Gettysburg and were captured at Chattanooga. Now, here in Andersonville prison, Billy's death meant that they were separated for the first time in their lives.

A light musical sound was carried on the air. John recognized it immediately as the sweet chimes of Billy's watch, the watch his father had given him when he left to join his regiment, the watch he had promised to John if anything should happen to him. John looked up. A Confederate guard was leering down at him from one of the pigeon coops. The watch was in his hand. The lid was opened and the chimes floated on the wind.

'Need the dead cart down there?' the guard called. John recognized the Alabama drawl. 'Looks to me like you Yankee boys ain't so good at stayin' alive.'

John turned away. He heard the guard calling out for the dead cart, but wouldn't give him the satisfaction of looking up at him again.

'Know that guard's name?' John turned to the other prisoner.

'That's the Preacher. I seen 'im shoot a defenceless man and quote from the scriptures at the same time. You keep away from him.'

'He was with someone.'

'That'll be his brother. Dangerous-crazy, both of 'em.

9

They been robbin' prisoners since this hell hole was put here. Ain't nothin' no one can do about it.'

'He killed my friend,' John said. 'He's holdin' his watch right now.'

John heard the Preacher laughing. 'Looks like you need the dead cart down there. I called 'im for you, Yankee boy.'

'Just walk away now,' the prisoner advised. 'Don't let his interest settle on you.'

John turned and made his way through the rows of tents to where Mikey was camped out on the ground. He pictured the Preacher's leering face. Right then and there, he vowed never to forget it.

1

Minnesota Territories. Seven Years Later. — 1871

A woman sat on the porch of the farmhouse smoking a cob pipe. She was in her late thirties. Her dark hair was turning grey and her handsome face was lined. Her dark skin showed Sioux blood a generation back. She was pregnant, barely two months gone. It was evening. She was watching her son trying to corral the goats into the pen for the night and laughing at his efforts to get them to move.

The boy was fourteen. He was tall and handsome like his mother. He had her challenge in his eyes. He knew it amused his mother to watch him struggling with the goats and he enjoyed putting on a show to entertain her.

'Leave her be, William,' she called to him. 'Your father will get her in when he gets home.'

The boy's face soured. 'He ain't my pa. Can't you stop callin' him that?'

The woman got up from her seat and stepped into the house, as if she hadn't heard him.

'You get yourself washed up. Supper's almost ready.'

The boy struggled on with the nanny goat for a while and then gave up. He walked over to the well in front of the house, hauled up a bucket and splashed icy water on his face and hands. Chickens pecked at the dirt round his feet.

Night fell swiftly here. As soon as the sun touched the peaks of the Black Hills away to the west, shadows began to lengthen. Now, colour was beginning to drain out of the day. William stayed sitting on the edge of the well, not wanting to go inside to be alone with his mother until he was called. He looked to the south, over the fields of corn stubble. They had harvested last week. It was another poor year. They would have to buy in hay to see the horses through the winter. The summer sun had baked the ground; they had had months without rain. Their few stooks stood in a row. The stems were almost white and the ears were blackened. In spite of this, William had enjoyed the harvest. He was big enough to swing the heavy scythe this year and could see the part of the field for which he had been responsible.

'William,' his mother called from inside the house. 'Come on in now. We'll start without him.'

William noticed that she had not used his stepfather's name. He waited for a moment and then slid down off the side of the well and began to walk towards the barn.

'Just checkin' the horses,' he called.

After a cursory glance inside the barn, William pushed the door closed and put the heavy wooden bar across it.

Inside the house, an oil lamp was already lit. William knew his mother had lit it early, before it was really dark, to make the room inviting for him. She stood at the chimney and ladled thin stew out of a pot which hung over the fire. William took his place at the table. His mother put down bowls of stew and the remains of a loaf in front of them. William bowed his head and waited for her to say grace.

'No,' his mother said. 'You say grace, William, as he's not here.'

Again, William noticed how his mother had avoided using his stepfather's name. He mumbled grace quickly and started to eat.

'Where is he?' William said.

'He went out to set traps in the woods above the north pasture this afternoon. It's not like him to be away after nightfall.' She took a spoonful of food quickly.

'Want me to ride out?' William said. 'I kin find my way in the dark.'

His mother hesitated. 'We were going to do your Bible-reading after supper, William. You know we'd agreed that.'

William stared down into his food.

'What if he—?' William began.

'I know, we'll finish supper and wait a little while longer. He'll most likely be back by then.'

After supper, they went round the back of the house and hollered in the direction of the north pasture. They had done this before. On a still night, it was possible for their voices to carry for over a mile. But tonight, an east wind was getting up and snatched their words away.

'Let me go, Ma,' William said. 'I'll take Runaway. She knows the way.'

His mother hesitated. 'Ride up to the edge of the pasture and call from there. Wear your coat. It's a cold wind.'

William ran to the barn and saddled up the horse. His mother went inside to fetch a coat for him.

'Just go to the edge of the pasture. Don't go into the woods. A horse can stumble in the dark. It ain't fair on her. If you don't hear no answer, you come straight back, you understand. We'll both go up there at first light.'

13

'Can I take the shotgun, Ma?'

'What d'you want that for? There ain't no need.'

His mother saw the pride in her son's face at being allowed to go out on the search. She heard the urgency in his voice.

'I dunno, Ma. Can I take it?'

'All right. But don't you go shootin' at shadows and wastin' shells.'

'I know, Ma. It's just to have it with me.'

William slipped down out of his saddle and sprinted into the house to fetch the gun from its place on the chimney breast.

'Don't you be long, now.' She rested her hand on her pregnant belly. 'I mean it. You know I ain't good on my own.'

William turned to her. 'Don't you worry none, Ma.' He clicked his tongue and the horse moved forward.

'Start shouting out before you get to the edge of the pasture,' she called.

The wind swirled, carrying with it the first few autumn leaves. The temperature had suddenly dropped. She hurried towards the house, not knowing whether he had heard her. From the shelter of the porch, she stared after her son but the darkness had swallowed him.

Inside the house, the woman cleared away the dishes and stacked them in a skillet ready for washing at the well in the morning. Moving a chair close to the fire, she took a cob pipe and a pouch of home-grown tobacco from the pocket of her apron. She began to read from a Bible open on her lap while she stuffed the dry leaves into the bowl of the pipe. The Song of Solomon. The musical words entered into her head and soothed away the anxiety about her husband and her son and together with the rich smoke that filled her lungs, put her at ease.

Suddenly, after a while reading, the woman realized too much time had gone by. She snapped the Bible shut, jumped to her feet and stepped quickly over to the door. She peered out into the night. The wind was blowing harder, slinging leaves and dust against the cabin. Worry clawed within her. Too agitated to read, she checked the level of oil in the lamp and stacked two more logs on the fire. Outside, the wind wailed.

William must have gone on into the woods in spite of what she had said. She was angry with him and fearful for him at the same time. It would be easy for the horse to stumble and throw him. Don't think like that. The boy rides well. He had looked so proud and excited as he mounted up. She couldn't have stopped him. He was growing up too fast.

The woman caught herself pacing the room, made herself stop and sit down by the fire again. But this time it was too hot and she moved her chair away. It was impossible to settle to reading. Faces reared and disappeared in the dancing flames. She spread the palm of her hand over her pregnant belly for comfort, still waiting to feel the baby move for the first time.

A loud, angry hammering on the door made her jump out of her seat. Fear lanced through her. Up on the chimney breast, the hooks which had supported the shotgun were empty. She stared around the room looking for something to defend herself with. A kitchen knife. The poker. She picked up the poker and put it down again, not knowing what to do and called out. A man's voice answered, but she couldn't make out the words against the scream of the wind.

She opened the door ajar. The sudden draught made the flames in the fireplace flare to one side and lurch out into the room. Two men pushed their way in. They wore heavy coats and hats pulled low against the weather.

' 'Scuse us, ma'am. It ain't a night to be standin' in the porch, is it now?'

She was afraid, but hid her fear deep within her.

'Surely ain't. You gentlemen just travellin' through? You're welcome to warm yourselves by the fire.' She tried to sound relaxed but knew the men would hear the worry in her voice.

The men took off their hats and knocked the rain off them on to the floor.

'We're lookin' for John Wright. We was tol' this was his place.' The first man looked at her with cold, expressionless eyes. He smiled as he spoke. 'We was together in Andersonville. Mikey Donnal. This here's me cousin Sean.'

'This is John's house. He'll be back soon. He's mentioned your names,' she said. She gestured them to sit by the fire. The men thanked her and pulled chairs nearer the warmth. Mikey reached down and shoved another log on the blaze.

'John's a good man,' Mikey continued. 'I asked around in Calamity yesterday, but no one seems to know him. Only the old fella at the store. John keeps himself to himself out here, I guess.'

'We don't care to go into town much. Only to pick up supplies.'

'Me an' Sean helped John out in Andersonville. You could say we saved his life. We hid him when the guards were looking for him.'

'I know it was a terrible place,' she said. 'John doesn't

16

like to speak of it.' Mikey rubbed his hands over the fire.

'I can offer you a bowl of soup.'

Both men thanked her. She stood between them, ladling the food from the pot over the fire. She felt uneasy, having to stand so close to them. Sean moved his chair back to let her pass. The wind moaned round the eaves of the house and drew the flames hard up the chimney.

'Forgive me for askin',' Mikey said, 'you're John's wife?'

She looked at him sharply. 'Yes, I'm Hannah,' she said. 'Of course. What were you thinkin'?'

Mikey smiled. 'It's just—'

'That I'm older than him?'

'Then that'll be his child you're carryin'.'

Hannah blushed.

'John got any other children?'

'I have a son. He's out lookin' for John now, in the north pasture.'

Mikey laughed. 'What's he doin' out after dark? The wind's up.'

Fear stabbed through her. 'He's late,' she said. 'He was settin' traps in the woods.'

'Somethin' happened to him?' Mikey looked at her closely.

'No. Horse got lame, I expect.' She felt for her pipe in the pocket of her apron. 'He'll be back soon. They both will.' She sat down at the table away from the fire while the men ate.

'Mighty nice soup, ma'm,' Sean said. He spoke louder than was necessary. 'We stayed over last night at Calamity. Only thing we could get to eat was dry biscuits. Before that we was on the trail. I had enough trail food to last me a lifetime.'

'John's got a goodly spread up here,' Mikey said. 'He's done well for himself since the war.'

'This is my place,' Hannah said. 'Me an' my husband built it up. It ain't no goodly spread neither. The house is strong but the farm don't yield. Snow all winter, hot as a furnace all summer.'

'You a widow-woman?' Mikey said. His eyes watched her carefully and his enquiry sounded innocent.

'I ain't,' Hannah said. 'Me an' my husband parted.' She changed the subject. 'Looks like you fellas will be wantin' to stay the night. Why don't you put your horses in the barn. There's feed over there. You can bed down on the straw later, when you've seen John.'

She took the soup bowls from them and put them in the skillet with the others. Sean got to his feet.

'You go on,' Mikey said. 'Find some straw for us.' He turned to Hannah. 'Would you mind fetchin' me a drink of water, missus? There was a fair bit o' salt in that stew.'

She heard the criticism of her cooking but did not respond to it. She got up from the table and filled a tin mug with water from a pan.

'So how long has John and you bin together?'

'Since the spring, the year after the war,' Hannah said.

'He's a lucky young fella,' Mikey smiled. 'Though you're nearer my age, I reckon.' Hannah looked at him.

'I'm just sayin'. I'm thirty-eight years. I know John was twenty when we was in Andersonville; that would make him twenty-seven now. Sure landed on his feet when he took up with you an' all. I mean, what with the farm.'

'This is Wilderness County, Minnesota, mister. We just concentrate on survivin' up here. A few years don't mean nothing.'

'Looks like you're doin' well for yourselves,' Mikey continued in his musical voice. 'I mean, you gotta understan', the war was hell. Me an' Sean was in Andersonville for a year. I know about survivin'. I know what you gotta do.' He paused. 'John's got a young man's strength for the farm. You ain't gonna have no trouble with the Injuns, what with you bein' half Injun yourself. You're doin' well fer yourselves, is what I'm sayin'.'

Hannah rested her hand on her belly and stood by the fire and watched him. The wind whined outside the house like a wounded animal.

'I mean, me an' Sean went back to Five Points after the army. But if you know Five Points, you know there wasn't a whole lot there to start with, so there wasn't a whole lot to go back to. We lit out for the territories, same as John musta done. Only thing is we went south to cattle country, while he come north to Minnesota. Cowboyin', now that is real hard work. Us Five Points boys, we ain't cut out for cowboyin', that's fer sure. We just ended up driftin' from place to place.'

Mikey chuckled to himself and sat back in his chair.

'If I'd come north, it could be me up in the woods by the north pasture on a windy night, right now. Could be my child in your belly. Just think o' that.'

Hannah turned away from him. 'There ain't no way, mister.'

'I was just supposin'. I didn't mean nothin' by it. It's just chance, is all. North, south. What we do. It's just a change in the wind.'

Mikey watched her.

'After that, everythin' comes to survival,' he continued. 'Don't matter if you're in some Johnny Reb prison camp, if you're in Five Points, New York or if you're in Wilderness County, Minnesota. You jest do the best you can to stay alive.' He paused. 'I helped your boy John survive. When that guard cut his fingers off, I bandaged up his han' otherwise he would have bled to death. I hid 'im so them Johnny Reb scum couldn't find 'im. Least till they got tired of lookin'. You wouldn't have 'im if it wasn't for me.'

She had never seen such anger disguised by a smiling face, she thought. The wind moaned in the chimney like a lament for the dead.

'I'm grateful you did that,' Hannah said.

Mikey looked at her as if she had conceded something and he sensed an advantage. He smiled. 'Sure you are.'

'Hadn't you best be seein' to your horse?' Hannah asked.

'Sean'll do it. He loves horses. Prefers 'em to people, I reckon,' Mikey laughed. 'You got anythin' to drink around here?'

'No,' she said. 'Not without John here.'

Mikey sighed. 'We could have a drink. Why not? He wouldn't mind.'

A shot sounded outside. They both looked towards the door. Mikey leapt to his feet and drew his Colt. He gestured Hannah to move to the side of the room. He cocked his Colt and aimed it at the door.

There was a footstep on the porch and the door burst open. William hurled himself into the room.

Hannah threw herself on Mikey's arm and his shot went into the floor.

'Ma,' William screamed, 'there was a man in the barn. I shot 'im.'

William stood in the doorway framed against the darkness. The draught grabbed the flames from the fireplace

20

and hurled them sideways.

'He was stealing the horses, Ma.'

Mikey holstered his gun, shoved William aside and dashed out into the night.

2

John slumped down at the base of an oak tree and turned up the collar of his coat. His dead horse lay beside him. The wind in the branches high above sounded like the sea. A pile of squirrel and fox carcasses which had been caught in the traps lay at his feet. He was still holding his gun.

John had raised Blackie from a foal. He had bought her from a dealer passing through Calamity the first year he lived there, broken her and trained her himself. He knew he shouldn't have stayed out in the woods in the poor evening light. When the horse stumbled, John thought it had tripped on a branch and that the crack he heard was the branch breaking.

The horse went down, threw John and the pile of animal carcasses he had slung across the saddle. The animal screamed and kicked out. John knew then. And by the way she didn't immediately struggle back on to her feet. After a while she lay still. John was able to examine her. A spear of white bone stuck out through the skin of her left front leg. He shot her right away.

After a few minutes, John got to his feet. He was five miles from home, deep in the woods. The wind was up and it was dark. He would come back with William in the morning, bury the horse and collect the saddle. He slung the heavy bundle of carcasses across his shoulder, regretting now that he had not skinned them at the traps, and started for home.

He stumbled over tree roots and the uneven ground. The sound of the wind beating in the high trees and the gathering darkness disorientated him. The woods, which he knew so well in daylight became a foreign place. He walked slowly. The carcasses weighed heavy across his shoulders. At times, he thought he was walking in circles. The path was ill defined in daylight, by night it was impossible to follow.

Eventually, he came to the tree-line at the top of the north pasture. The slope of the ground led him in the direction he had to go. Clouds covered the stars and there was no moon. The wind danced around him like a boxer.

Walking was harder here than in the woods. John pushed on until he thought he could make out a faint speck of light below, away to the right. It gave him a bearing. The pinprick of light flickered in the darkness. There was no fixed, still point. The wind seemed to blow his vision from side to side. The light was there, then it was not. Then it disappeared altogether.

'I killed him, Ma.' The boy's face broke with anguish. 'He's lyin' by the stalls an' he ain't movin'.'

Hannah drew her son to her. He set the shotgun down on the table and threw his arms around her, burying his head in her breast. She held him while he sobbed.

'I thought he was stealin' the horses, Ma.'

'Hush now,' she said. 'You sit by the fire.'

'Who was that man in here?'

'They're friends of John's,' she said. 'From the war.'

23

'I thought he was stealin' the horses, Ma. I asked him what he was doin'. He never answered me.'

William started crying again; tears of shock and fear.

Hannah led him to the chair by the fire and sat him down.

'I'm going out to the barn,' she said.

She picked up the oil lamp and cupped her hand over it to protect the flame. It did no good. As soon as she opened the door the fire reared in the grate and the lamp blew out. She closed the door, set the lamp on the table and went to fetch a spill to relight it from the fire. Her shadow danced over the ceiling as she stooped at the grate.

The door was flung open, practically torn off its hinges. Mikey stood there, his gun in his hand. Orange flames leapt up from the hearth. Black shadows careered round the room.

He sprang at William and hauled him to his feet. William offered no resistance and seemed to hang in Mikey's hand like a broken doll. Mikey pressed his Colt against William's temple. Red firelight jumped across his face.

'Lucky for you, boy, he ain't dead. He sure is bleedin' bad.'

He glared at William, tightening his grip on his collar and cocked the gun. He turned to Hannah.

'You didn't even come out to the barn. What kinda heartless creature are you?' His voice rose to a scream. 'Ain't you got no bandages? Can't you get out there and tend to him?'

Terrified, Hannah stared at the gun pointed at her son's head. Mikey's words seemed to break her trance.

'Yes, yes,' she said. 'Bandages. I'll look after him.'

She pulled a wooden chest from under the bed. In it were rolled strips of cotton and a few blue glass bottles. She quickly gathered up some of them.

'Please, mister,' she pleaded. 'I'll see to your friend. The boy never meant no harm.'

'Get out there and stop the bleedin',' Mikey screamed.

Hannah ran to the barn.

Mikey shook William, choking him, and then threw him down in the chair. William gasped for air. Mikey shoved the barrel of his gun up against William's windpipe. 'You better be prayin' he stays alive. Otherwise, you gonna be doin' a lotta screamin' before you die.'

He took the gun slowly from the boy's neck and shoved it back in its holster. William stared at him, not daring to move. Mikey's eyes burned like live coals.

In the barn, Hannah had lit the stub of a candle and set it on the earth floor beside Sean. She had taken off his jacket and gunbelt and pulled his shirt away from the wound. His right side looked as though it had been gnawed by a dog. Buckshot peppered his chest and arm.

Hannah splashed alcohol over the wound, folded the strips of cotton into a pad and bound it against his side where the flesh was ripped away. She would have to dig the shot out in the morning.

Mikey appeared beside her. 'How's he doin?'

'Gotta keep him warm.' She rested the palm of her hand on Sean's forehead. 'Shock's makin' him cold.'

'I'll carry 'im in by the fire,' Mikey said.

Hannah nodded agreement.

Mikey stooped down and picked the man up.

'Gently,' Hannah said. 'You'll open up the wounds.'

She ran ahead and held the door to the barn and then the door to the house.

'He ain't dead?' William said.

'No, he ain't,' Hannah said. 'Build up the fire. We gotta keep the place real warm for him.'

Mikey laid Sean down on the bed in the corner of the room. There was an Indian blanket laid across it. He pulled it over Sean and took off his boots.

'I'll make some coffee,' Hannah said. 'Light the lamp please, William.'

Mikey sat down at the table. Hannah set the coffee pot on the hearth. William hung back in the shadows at the edge of the room.

'Did you see a sign of John, William?' Hannah said. She spoke in a whisper, kneeling in front to the fire with her back to him.

'No,' he said. 'I called out, but I couldn't hear nothin' in the wind.'

Mikey looked up at him. 'Did ya call out to Sean in the barn?'

'Yeah, I did, mister. He didn't say nothin'. He just carried on. He was goin' round all our horses. He just ignored me like I wasn't there.'

'So you shot 'im.'

'I guess. I reckoned he was after stealin' our horses.'

'You didn't walk round in front o' him, to make sure he seed you? Nothin' like that.'

'No. I was by the door.'

'You young crackerjack,' Mikey sneered. 'He's deaf. He was stood next to a cannon at Bull Run when it went off. Ain't heard nothin' since.'

'I'm sorry, mister. I just thought he was stealin' our horses.' William looked as though he was going to cry again.

Mikey ignored him. He looked at Hannah. 'Way I look at it is, you owe me. First, I save John from some crazy Johnny

26

Reb guard in Andersonville; then I ride all the way up here to give him some information which I know he'd be anxious to have; third, this fool kid shoots my cousin Sean.'

Hannah stood by the fire. 'What information?'

'Information is for my army buddy. It's a business proposition. It ain't for his squaw.'

Hannah flinched. 'Don't call me that.'

'I'll call you whatever I want to,' Mikey snapped. 'I'm considerin' exactly what favours you're gonna do for me, you being in my debt an' all.' He turned to William. 'One squeak outa you, I'm gonna rip your spine out. Now, where's that coffee?'

The flames leapt again as the door opened. John stood in the doorway. He was whey-faced and exhausted. His jacket was covered in mud and blood from the carcasses. Mikey leapt to his feet. William ran to him and threw his arms round him.

'Pa.'

'Hey,' John said. 'What's all this?'

He dropped the heap of carcasses by the door. Then he saw Mikey, with the flames playing behind him. He walked over to embrace him, but Mikey stood motionless as John clasped him.

Hannah pulled a second chair up to the fire for John and poured coffee for them all. She sat at the bedside and watched over Sean, leaving the men to talk. William sat with her.

Mikey recounted the events of the evening.

'My horse caught its foot in a rabbit hole an' broke its leg,' John said. 'I had to shoot her and walk back, otherwise I woulda been here.'

'I'm trustin' that your woman knows what she's doin an'

27

she ain't gonna let Sean die on me,' Mikey said.

'He won't die,' Hannah said. 'He just needs rest and time to heal. I've stopped the bleedin'. Buckshot'll have to be picked out in the mornin' when there's a good light.'

'Maybe she knows some o' them Injun remedies.' Mikey spoke across her.

'Why did you come here?' John said.

Mikey looked at him. 'We found your man,' he said. 'The Preacher. I got a proposition for you.' John was silent.

'I went back to New York after the war but there weren't no reason to stay,' Mikey continued. 'Then we heard that Wirtz was on trial.'

'Wirtz?' John said.

'Captain Henry Wirtz, Commander of Andersonville. Had 'im up in front of a military tribunal. Found 'im guilty an' hanged 'im too,' Mikey said, 'for impairing the health an' destroying the lives of prisoners. War crimes, they called it.' Mikey spat into the fire. 'I saw that dirty reb captain every day we was in Andersonville. He rode round the dead line every mornin' with his pack o' dogs followin' on behind. He would just look at us, like he was seein' us an' not seein' us.'

'I saw 'im,' John said. 'We all did.'

'Wirtz never did no harm to nobody himself. Got his men to do it for him. But the Preacher an' his stinkin' Johnny Reb brothers an' the others, now that's a different story. I seed 'em shoot men an' leave 'em dyin' on the ground. I seen 'em hang fellas. I seen 'em throw fellas over the dead line so's the guards in the pigeon coops would use 'em for target practice.' Mikey was shaking. 'I seed 'em hang a young guy up by his thumbs once. Left 'im there all night, screamin'. In the mornin' they cut 'im down and shot

28

'im in the chest. Took 'im a day an' a half to die.'

'I know all these things,' John said. 'I seen 'em too. I don't like to think of it, nor speak of it neither.'

Mikey laughed. 'Well, why would you? You got your farm an' your Injun wife. I mean, she says she's your wife. Church married, are you?'

'No,' John said quietly. 'We ain't.'

'Well then,' Mikey jeered. 'You got some other fella's wife. Some other fella's farm. Your nice comfortable life. Why should you care about what's right? Takes an Irish boy from Five Points to do that, don' it?'

'What d'you mean?'

'While you been sittin' pretty up here on your farm, I bin trackin' down them sonsabitches that did that to us in Andersonville. I found three of 'em already. Remember that tall, mean one that used to shoot into the crowd of prisoners whenever he felt bored?'

'Yeah, I remember him.'

'Found 'im in Richmond. Livin' there all nice with his wife an' kid.' Mikey laughed. 'Well, he ain't livin' there no more. There or no place. He was screamin' in Hell before he died, with 'is pretty Southern wife watchin'.'

The wind moaned round the house. Mikey threw another log on the fire and sparks showered out.

'Now I found the Preacher,' he said 'and his stinkin' brother. He killed your frien', didn't he?'

'Where?' John asked

'They'll be just south o' Reckless right about now. They've joined a wagon train headin' West. Rode over two hundred miles to tell ya.'

Mikey smiled.

'Made it without getting shot at too, till we got here.'

29

Mikey glowered at William.

The door rattled in the wind, as if someone were trying to get in. The oil lamp flickered and the fire danced. Hannah put her arm around William's shoulder.

Mikey turned to Hannah. 'He tell you about all this?'

Hannah shook her head.

'War's over,' John said. 'It's best left that way.'

Mikey looked at him coldly. 'I'm from Five Points. An eye for an eye.' He looked over at William. 'You believe in an eye for an eye, don'tcha, boy?'

William stared at the floor and didn't answer.

'Figured you might be interested in this,' Mikey said. He reached inside his jacket, brought out a newspaper and tossed it on the table.

'Read it out to me,' John said. He looked at Hannah.

'It's a news story. Says the Preacher had himself a business sellin' guns to the Comanche down in Texas. There's a bounty on his head of a thousand dollars. I figured that as he had a brother who is just as murderous as he is, me an' Sean needed a third man. So we thought of you.' He looked around the room. 'Sure looks as though you could do with the money.' Mikey studied John, watching for his reaction.

'Them Winchesters he sold,' Mikey continued, 'they killed Yankee troopers. Wiped out a whole regiment. Then the savages scalped every single one of 'em, so I heard. Left their brains fryin' in the desert sun.'

John recoiled at the thought. Mikey got up and walked over to look down at Sean.

'His temperature's good and he's breathing regular,' Hannah said. 'He's sleeping now.'

'I never figured myself for a bounty hunter,' John said. He stared into the fire. Mikey idly ran his hand over

Hannah's shoulder as he stood beside her. She looked at him sharply and moved away from him.

Mikey turned to John. 'A thousand dollars is a lot o' money, even split. You'd get paid for bringin' in the guy that killed your frien'. Paper says dead or alive. Sure gonna need ya now your boy shot Sean.' Mikey laughed.

'Anyhow, time we was gettin' some shut-eye. Looks like Sean's got your bed for the night. You and the boy can bed down in here. I'll take the squaw out to the barn with me.'

'You watch your mouth.' John's voice was steel. 'You might have come here, mister, just remember you wasn't invited.'

Mikey laughed. He picked up his hat and jacket before heading out to sleep in the barn.

'You got a bottle I could nurse out there, to keep the cold out?'

John nodded to Hannah who searched in the back of a cupboard and found a half-empty bottle of corn whiskey.

John said, 'We'll figure what we're gonna do in the morning.'

3

John and William left for the woods at first light. They saw Mikey sprawled asleep in the barn when they collected the horses. Sean's blood had left a dark stain on the yellow hay. Mikey didn't wake. The empty bottle lay beside him. The wind had blown itself out in the night and the day was calm. They took a pick and shovels.

'You gonna go with 'im, Pa?' William asked, as they rode across the pasture towards the woods.

'I'm thinkin' on it,' John said. He stared straight ahead of him. 'I got you to look after your ma. She'll tell you what needs doin' on the farm.'

'I know that anyway,' William said.

They rode in silence. The morning air was cool on their faces. Up ahead, the leaves on the maple trees at the forest edge were turning orange at the approach of autumn. A meadow lark glided above them, a flash of gold against the pale sky. Jack-rabbits played in the oat grass and a young white-tailed deer showed itself for a moment between the trees.

'How long will you be gone?' William persisted.

John reflected. 'Three weeks, a month. I'll be back before the snows come.'

'It'll be dangerous, won't it? This Preacher, he's a killer, ain't he?'

John looked at the boy. 'Mikey'll be with me. He wants the bounty as much as I do. Anyways, if I got a chance to bring Billy's murderer to justice, I gotta go. And if we don't get some money, I don't know how we're gonna get through next year. We're gonna be relyin' on the traps again.'

They came to the edge of the woods.

'Reckon we should leave the horses here,' John said. 'Sure can't afford to lose another one.' They dismounted and untied the pick and shovels from their saddles.

'It ain't far to walk.'

Hannah boiled up a pan of water with a pair of tweezers and a knife in it and found another bottle of red eye.

'You gonna let me drink a mouthful o' that?' Sean said.

Hannah passed him the bottle then went to work. Sean gripped the side of the bed and grunted with pain. The pieces of buckshot rattled round a tin cup as she picked them out.

She looked Sean directly in the eye. 'Wound's clean,' she said. She splashed red eye on it and bandaged it again.

Mikey pushed open the door.

'John's up in the woods buryin' his horse,' Hannah said briefly.

'I never said I was lookin' for him,' Mikey said. 'Cup o' coffee an' a little female company would be a grand way to start the day.'

Hannah nodded towards where the coffee pot stood at the edge of the fire. She corked the whiskey and tucked the bottle away at the back of the cupboard. Mikey picked up the cup containing the buckshot. 'Fifteen,' he counted.

'And a whole load more took a piece outa him. Good thing that boy o' yours is a lousy shot, or he mighta done some damage.'

Mikey tipped the buckshot out on to the table and filled the cup with coffee.

'Don't you eat in the mornin'?'

'There's some soup left from yesterday if you're hungry,' Hannah said. 'I ain't skinned the squirrels yet, nor cleaned 'em. We'll be havin' them tonight, I guess.'

'I ain't partial to squirrel,' Mikey said. 'Reminds me too much o' the rat meat we used to have in Andersonville. 'Course, that was a luxury then.'

Hannah took the animal carcasses out on to the porch to skin them. Mikey stayed inside to talk to Sean.

It was mid-afternoon when John and William returned. Mikey was sitting on the porch, Hannah was inside, inventing chores for herself and avoiding him.

'We'll have to stop in Calamity to pick up supplies,' Mikey announced later. 'You ain't got nothin' to spare here. I can see that.'

'I ain't got money for supplies,' John said.

'Don't you worry about that,' Mikey said. 'It won't cost you nothin'.'

John brightened at generosity he had not expected.

'Just pleased to have you along. I thought for a moment, the Injun was gonna stop you from comin',' he reflected. 'I seed that before: a man ruled by a woman. Not when the woman was a half-breed, of course.'

Hannah was inside and hadn't heard. John let it go.

Mikey grinned at him. 'Gonna be like old times.'

'If we leave early this evenin', we could ride more'n ten

miles before sundown,' Mikey said. 'Up at first light, we'd be in Calamity early in the morning. Stores'd just be openin' up. We could pick up supplies an' be on our way with the horses still fresh. If we wait till tomorrow mornin' to leave, it'll be evenin' time before we get to the town. Then we'd have to wait till the next day before we got the supplies.'

Hannah watched as Sean protested that he was not up to the ride and needed another couple of days' rest. Mikey would have none of it. He convinced him that a short ride that evening which allowed them to break the journey to Calamity was best. Hannah gave Sean all her remaining cotton bandages and told him to pack the wound tight if the bleeding started again.

John buckled on his gunbelt and took William to one side.

'When you go up to the woods to set the traps, you take the rifle with you. You might see a deer. If you do, hold the rifle tight against your shoulder and aim for the head. That way, you'll drop it right away. If you hit it in the body, it'll run on for miles an' you'll never catch it. You'll have to get your ma up there to skin it. Don't you try that by yourself, you understand?'

'I know, Pa,' William said.

'You keep your eye out for a deer. I'm reckonin' you'll be runnin' out of food pretty soon.

'And another thing. The hay. What there is of it.'

'I know,' William said. 'Let it dry out then get it in the barn. If it rains, get it in anyway.'

'And keep turnin' it. Every day.'

'I know, Pa.'

'If it starts to go mouldy, separate that off from the rest.

Take it outside and burn it.'

'Pa,' William said, 'I can do it. I'll look after everythin'.'

John put his arm around the boy's shoulders and drew him close.

'I know you will.'

Mikey helped Sean saddle his horse in the barn. John and Hannah sat on the porch waiting for them. William had saddled John's horse and tethered it to the rail.

'Sean ain't fit enough to ride,' Hannah said.

She fell silent and stared out over the parched field. John sensed her unease.

'I gotta go,' John said. 'A thousand dollars. The farm's gone to hell this year. Snow all winter, drought all summer. I ain't got a choice.'

'There's always a choice,' she said. Her voice was calm and without judgement.

'I know you don't like 'im.'

'That doesn't matter,' she said. 'You want to do this, that's enough.'

'It's for the farm. For all of us. And for Billy. I gotta.'

'I know,' Hannah said.

Hawks wheeled over them, soaring and diving in the air.

'Birds are getting ready to go south,' she said. 'Maybe winter's comin' early.'

'I'll be back before the snows. A month, that's all.'

She rested her hand on her pregnant belly. John placed his hand on top of hers.

'Before the snows,' he said. 'You'll see.'

Mikey and Sean rode out from the barn. John left Hannah's side and mounted up. William slipped into the seat beside his mother on the porch. John turned towards them and waved one last time. William called out goodbye as the three men headed south. High above them, the hawks zigzagged. The crests of the Black Hills were lit by the golden sun.

That evening, the men made camp by boxthorn trees. There was a pool there, but the water was stagnant. The rotting carcass of a coyote lay half in the water and a veil of storm flies had settled on it. It was almost dark, too late to move on anywhere else. The men moved their bedrolls upwind of the carcass. John gathered dry wood and made a fire. He had brought coffee and hard tack.

They had covered more ground than they thought though. Sean's wounds hadn't opened up much. They would be in Calamity inside of two hours in the morning.

'Hard day's ride tomorrow,' Mikey said. 'We'll be wantin' to put as much ground between us an' Calamity as we can.' He looked at Sean. 'Be ready.'

The morning was bright and clear as the three of them rode in to town. They headed straight for the saloon to have breakfast. Mikey chose a table by the window which looked out on to the grocery store, the barber's shop and the bank across the street. They ate bacon and potatoes and watched the townsfolk prepare for the day. They saw the owner of the grocery store unlock the door and hook back the shutters. The barber opened up his shop and took his first customer, a wild-looking frontiersman in a buckskin jacket with steel-grey hair and a beard. Mikey ordered more coffee.

Calamity was a small trading town. The stores carried supplies and equipment for the few local sodbusters and the men who worked the mining claims on the eastern slopes of the Black Hills. If they ever found gold, the bank exchanged it for cash.

After they had seen a Wells, Fargo coach leave and a clerk in shirtsleeves and an eye-shade unbolt the door to the bank, Mikey left a few coins on the bar to pay for the breakfasts. They crossed the street to the grocery store and bought beans, hard tack biscuits and coffee for the trail. Mikey appeared to have run out of money and argued about the price, making out that the supplies were overpriced, which they clearly weren't. Eventually, the store-keeper gave him a reduction.

When they had tied the supplies on to their saddles, Mikey told John to water the horses at a trough behind the store. He said he and Sean had forgotten to buy tobacco and were going back for it. John led the three horses up the alley between the store and the bank.

John looked around for a water trough but there wasn't one there. There was a wooden fence running behind the buildings. He remembered seeing a trough outside the saloon. He turned around and began to lead the horses back again.

Gunshots ripped through the morning air. There was shouting from the street. Mikey and Sean came careering up the alley towards him.

'Turn round,' Mikey yelled. 'You can't come back down here.'

It took John a moment to realize that Mikey had his gun in one hand and a canvas bank bag in the other. Sean was running after him, bank bag in one hand and his weapon drawn.

Mikey grabbed the reins of his horse out of John's hand and hauled the animal to turn him round.

'Come on,' he yelled. He scrambled up into the saddle and jabbed his spurs into the horse's side. The animal leapt forward. Mikey barely had control as the animal careered up the alley.

John and Sean fought to turn their horses and mount up. The animals were startled at the sudden noise and confusion. John got up into the saddle and followed Mikey. He looked round. Sean grimaced with pain as he tried to pull himself up into the saddle, awkwardly holding the heavy bag and his gun. Blood soaked his shirt as the old wound broke. John urged his horse on. There was shouting from the street as he rounded the corner. Shots were fired. Mikey was up ahead spurring his horse into a gallop. Sean was tight behind him.

Then Mikey reined his horse in hard. The animal reared up and almost threw him. John realized what was happening just in time to draw in his own horse. Two men were dragging out a cart to block the path between the back of the buildings and the fence. Mikey pulled his horse hard right to cut down between two buildings to the main street. As he turned to follow Mikey, John saw the men crouch behind the wagon and draw their weapons.

Mikey charged out into the street. There was firing behind them from the men by the wagon. Bullets whined through the air and flicked splinters of wood off the sides of the buildings. John looked round. Sean was still with them, leaning to one side in his saddle.

They wheeled left in the street and spurred their horses on. Men were running out of the buildings, guns in their hands. Lead zipped past them through the clean morning air. Their horses took great leaping strides, wild-eyed, urged on by terror and confusion. Rifle shots volleyed after them.

They could see the edge of town up ahead. Staying low and clinging to the necks of their animals, they rode faster and faster towards the last buildings and the great empty plain to the south.

They galloped on past the last building, a grain ware-house. A man with a rifle stood up on the roof, taking careful aim. Mikey raised his Colt .45 as he galloped past and loosed off three shots. John saw the man fall two storeys on to the dirt road before he had had time to fire.

The riders thundered on over the plain towards the safety of the hills. Their hoofbeats drummed against the hard ground. The morning air bit the riders to the bone and the horses' manes lashed their faces. Their eyes streamed with tears.

John saw Mikey turn and look behind him. The hills were a mile ahead and the town was a mile behind. Mikey signalled to them and they slowed the horses. No one was following.

Mikey gave a great whoop and leapt down from his saddle, still clutching the bank bag. He tumbled to the ground and lay there laughing. John got down and strode over to him.

'Why didn't you tell me you were gonna do that?' he yelled. 'We didn't agree on robbin' a bank. What's got into you?'

Mikey sat up. 'Oh, you hush now. That was the best mornin's ride I had in a long while. Them fools back there couldn't shoot fish in a barrel neither.'

'What d'you do that for?' John's anger was still boiling in him.

'I said shut up. You'll get your share.' Mikey's voice was ice. 'Hey,' he added, 'you wanta see somethin' funny?' He reached into his pocket and brought out a crumpled ball of yellow paper. He smoothed it out and handed it to John. It was a wanted poster.

Wanted for Robberies and Unlawful Killing. Michael and Sean Donnal of Five Points, New York City. These men are wanted for crimes in the states of New York, Pennsylvania and Kentucky. Reward $1,000 payable by the Wells, Fargo bank on conviction for robbery and/or murder. The men are sometimes known as the Five Points Twins. They are believed to be headed into the western territories. Be on your guard. Signed Thomas Moines, Manager, Wells, Fargo Bank, Buffalo, New York.

'You never told me you was bank robbers,' John shouted. 'I don't want no share of a bank robbery. I ain't no thief. I came for reward money, honest an' legal.'

Mikey looked at him. 'Well,' he said, 'if you don't want your share, we'll be forced to take it for you. Ain't that so, Sean?'

Sean was still sitting on his horse, leaning to one side.

'Help me down, will ya?'

Mikey took Sean's weight as he lowered himself down from the saddle. Mikey turned to John.

'See what that fool boy of yours done?' Mikey spat.

Sean lay back, propping himself off the ground on an elbow. His shirt was soaked dark red. There were black shadows under his eyes.

'I caught one in the back, Mikey.' His words were made with the scrapings of breath.

Mikey bent close to hear him.

41

'Don't leave me, Mikey.'

'Don't be foolish,' Mikey blustered. 'Why should I leave you? What are you talkin' about?'

Blood from the back of Sean's shirt dripped down and formed pools in the dust. Mikey lifted the back. Hannah's bandages were dyed red. There was a dark bullet hole below his right shoulder-blade, above the bandages.

'Is it bad, Mikey?' Sean whispered.

Mikey looked at him in the face.

'There ain't nothin' there. No sign of nothin'. You ain't bin shot. I don't know what you're talkin' about.'

'You're kiddin' me,' Sean whispered. 'You're always kiddin', Mikey.'

'Wouldn't kid about a thing like that,' Sean said. 'We gotta get you on your horse an' get goin'. We'll find some place where we kin rest up awhile.'

John helped Mikey lift him back into the saddle. He was a deadweight and their hands were slippery with blood.

'Where's the money, Sean?' Mikey said.

'It's back a way, Mikey. I couldn't hold on to it. I let it fall.' Sean's face was ash and his voice was dust. 'Don't be angry with me, Mikey.'

Mikey turned his back on him.

'I ain't angry,' he said.

Mikey picked up his money bag, stuffed it in his saddle-bag and tied the flap down. He nodded to John and hauled himself into the saddle.

'Just as well you don't want no share of the money,' Mikey said. 'Sean just lost yours.'

He clicked his tongue and they started towards the hills.

4

Heading south out of Wilderness County, the men chose the hill climb rather than the river trail. It was a longer route but they would be able to look back and see if they were being followed. Inside of an hour, they were climbing the foothills of Pearl Mountain. It was almost midday. The sky was pale blue and cloudless. The rocky ground was scattered with thorn bushes and bluegrass. Higher up the slopes there were mountain maples and live oaks. The peak was spread with pines.

The horses picked their way over loose stones. They zigzagged up the slope until they came to a stand of oaks. Mikey reined in his horse.

'We get over this an' we're half way to Iowa,' he said.

They looked back across the plain. They could make out Calamity in the distance. Wisps of smoke rose from its chimneys and, from here, the collection of wooden buildings looked like something a child had made. There was no sign of a posse or anyone following them. Mikey seemed disappointed.

'I thought they woulda come after us. What with the reward money an' all.'

He laughed.

'We had 'em beat before we started. Man, that ride outa town was one o' the best I had. Yessir.'

Sean was leaning forward in his saddle. His face was twisted with pain. He refused John's offer to help him down. John passed him up a canteen of water and watched as he raised it with difficulty to his lips.

'If we ain't stoppin', we're goin',' Mikey said. 'You hang in there, Sean. You're doing just fine, Cousin.'

He clicked his tongue and guided his horse on up the slope.

After an hour, they came to a ridge. The slope to the west climbed steeply up to the mountain peak. Ahead of them, the wooded ground fell away. A couple of miles of forest led down to Paradise Lake. The leaves on the oaks and sugar maples were a sea of pale gold. Sunlight flashed on the surface of the water. The air tasted cool and sweet. An eagle soared above them, wheeling and circling, owner of the sky.

Sean was still slumped forward in his saddle. He held tight to the pommel to support himself. He turned his head to spit. His saliva was pink with blood. Mikey looked away. John offered him his canteen.

They made their way down through the woods. The canopy of branches obscured the sky. The light was smoky blue as if they were inside a high-roofed barn. Cottontail rabbits ran ahead of them. A white-tailed deer skittered away. A couple more hours, and the ground started to level out.

When the men emerged from the tree-line, they were at the shingle edge of the lake. The western shore was hidden in purple shadow as the sun moved towards the mountain peaks. A family of loons patrolled the water's edge close to where they stood. Their black and white markings disguised them against the light flickering on the surface. Their sharp, black beaks were ready to stab. Now and then, one would dive down without even breaking the surface of the water and emerge yards away, long after it seemed it must be lost.

'Mikey,' John said, 'reckon we should rest up.' He nodded towards Sean who was doubled over in his saddle. A shadow crossed Mikey's face.

'No,' Sean said, 'keep goin'. Jus' give me a drink of water.'

John held his canteen out to him. The effort of unclenching his hand from the saddle and stretching to take it was so painful for him that John thought he was going to fall.

'We should rest up,' John repeated.

'No,' Sean said. 'If I gotta get down from the saddle, my guts is gonna split open.' His voice was no more than a whisper.

Mikey urged his horse on down the lake shore. The others followed, a few yards behind, with John riding along-side Sean. The high, yodelling calls of the loons echoed over the water like the cries of lost souls.

At the far end of the lake, they walked into an ambush. Mikey heard a movement in the scrub to his right and turned. A volley of shots rang out. Winchesters and hand-guns. Bullets whined around them. Mikey wheeled his horse around and pushed past John, galloping back the way they had come. John hauled his own horse round, grabbed the bridle of Sean's horse and towed it after him.

'Come on,' he yelled to Sean. He galloped beside him, leaning over to pull the other horse's bridle along with him.

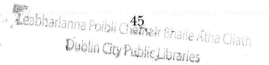

The shooting stopped. After a minute, they heard horses' hoofs chasing them. When they reached the far end of the lake, Mikey had already dismounted. His horse was hidden back beyond the tree-line and he was lying on the ground, his Winchester at his shoulder. As soon as John and Sean passed him, he fired. John jumped down off his horse and dived down beside Mikey. He reached for his Colt.

Three riders were heading for them like the wind. As soon as John and Sean started firing, they reined back their horses and swerved into the trees.

'Damn,' Mikey said. 'They gonna try an' work their way round behind us?'

He loosed off a few rounds.

'Give 'em time to get deeper into the woods. Then we kin make a run for it.'

'What about Sean?' John said.

'We can't stay here. We'll never see 'em comin' through the woods.'

They waited and listened. They heard men behind the tree-line. They couldn't see them nor tell how far away they were.

'Let's do it,' Mikey hissed.

They both slipped back into the trees and found their horses. Sean was doubled over in his saddle.

'You stick with me,' John said to him. Mikey looked round at them. John nodded.

Mikey dug his spurs in hard and his horse sprang out on to the lake shore. Mikey spurred him again and the horse surged forward until he was at full gallop. John's horse lunged after him. John had the reins of Sean's horse in his hand. They chased Mikey down the shore. There were some shots, but John couldn't tell where they came from. Mikey

46

rode with his gun in his hand.

When they reached the end of the shore again, two more men ran out of the woods. One of them raised a Winchester and took aim. The other one held a Colt. Mikey spurred his horse on and dropped down the right side of the saddle, holding on to the pommel with his left hand. The horse increased speed, and galloped straight at the men. Mikey fired again and again from down by the horse's neck, until the chamber was empty. The man aiming the Winchester flipped backwards with the force of the shots to his chest. He kicked the man beside him off balance and he fell into the lake in a crash of water.

Mikey only reined in his horse when they came to the end of the shore. They all halted and looked back. Mikey flicked open the chamber of his Colt and reloaded. The men who had gone into the woods were now back on the shore. They had seen what had happened and were keeping a safe distance. One of them took a few shots at them, but they went wide. They sat on their horses watching to see where Mikey led them.

'Whoo-ee. Mighty fine shootin', if I say so myself,' Mikey grinned. 'You see the way I did that? I never shot no one hanging off the saddle like that before.' He laughed. 'You see the way that fella went into the water?' He looked around for him. 'Where is he anyhow? I could take another shot at him.'

'Leave him,' John said. 'We gotta do something for Sean.'

'What can we do,' Mikey said, ' 'cept watch 'im die? It's kinda depressin'.'

'We gotta find a place where he can heal up up. We got supplies. It wouldn't do no harm to rest a few days. No one's gonna find us out here.'

'Those guys did. They ain't all dead neither. They're gonna be trailin' us every step we take. An' they're gonna send someone back to Calamity to get up a posse. We can't do no restin' up now.'

'Maybe they won't follow us today,' John said. 'Maybe they'll wait till morning.'

'You know as well as I do, they ain't gonna give up now,' Mikey said. 'Come on, we gotta cover as much ground as we can before dark.' He leaned over to Sean. 'You can keep going while there's daylight, can't you, Cousin?'

Sean was doubled over in the saddle and didn't answer.

Mikey clicked his tongue and his horse moved forward into the woods. At the trees John looked back. Further down the shore, the men were walking their horses towards them, keeping back out of range. John held the bridle of Sean's horse again and followed Mikey.

They reached the ridge above the lake as light began to fade. They were able to look back from here over the basin in which the lake lay. Somewhere down there in the woods were the men following them. Looking south, they could see open country. A great prairie lay between them and Reckless, the next town.

'I reckon they won't be so keen on following us tomorrow,' Mikey said, 'The reward ain't so big that they'll want to spend days away from home.'

'We gonna stop here?' John said.

'We got a vantage point here,' Mikey said. 'If we go on for an hour or two, then we'll end up halfway down the slope or out on the plain. We won't have no cover at all.'

They dismounted and lifted Sean out of his saddle. He cried out in agony as they held him. He was pale as ash,

48

sweating and cold. His shirt was crusted with dried blood. His wounds opened again when they moved him. Blood dripped off him on to the ground.

'Damnit, Cousin, you got more o' your blood on the outside than you have on the inside, I reckon,' Mikey said.

'Let me take a look,' John said.

Sean opened his eyes as John started to undo his shirt.

'No,' he said. 'Not right now. Just let me lie here a while.'

He smiled faintly and John covered him with his blanket and left him with his head resting on his saddle-bags, staring up at the sky.

Mikey sat on the edge of the ridge with his back to Sean, staring hard over the woods. John sat down beside him.

'Lookin' to see if I could spot 'em,' Mikey explained. 'But I can't see nothin'.'

The forest leaves shimmered gold and blood red in the dying sun. The surface of the lake was polished steel and the air was chill.

'Reckon they musta had someone who knows the territory real well to get ahead of us,' Mikey continued. 'I never expected that.'

'They could try it tomorrow,' John said. 'Could be tryin' to get ahead of us now.'

'They'd have to go back the way they come an' then circle round Pearl. That's a two-an'-a-half-day ride,' Mikey reflected. 'They know we're bound to head for Reckless. There ain't nowhere else to go. They'll try an' catch up with us there, I reckon.'

A pistol shot at close range split the air. A bullet ricocheted off the rock behind them. The family of loons beat their wings in alarm and lifted from the lake below them. Mikey and John threw themselves on the ground and grabbed their guns. They looked around desperately trying to see the shooter. Sean lay where they had left him. His gun was in his hand. A couple of feet behind Sean lay a dead rattlesnake with its head blown off.

It took John and Mikey a second to realize what had happened.

'Timber rattler,' Sean said. 'I seed 'im comin' for you, Mikey.' His voice was weak.

The thick body of the snake lay in the dust. The blotchy brown markings disguised it perfectly with the rock.

'Damn,' Mikey said. 'I never heard nothing.'

'I got 'im before he could get his rattle up,' Sean whispered.

Mikey picked up the snake and flung it down the hillside.

'Sure am grateful to you, Sean,' he said.

But Sean's eyes were closed. He was dead.

'Oh,' Mikey said, as if all the breath had been sucked out of him. He slumped down beside his cousin. He ran his hand over Sean's haggard face to close his eyes and pulled up the blanket to cover him.

John watched for signs of movement in the woods. Maybe the sound of the shot had let the pursuers know where they were. But there was nothing. Just the yellow leaves moving in the evening breeze, the surface of the lake shimmering in the remains of sunlight.

Mikey sat still and silent. Darkness gathered until it was barely possible to see the difference between the blackness of the trees and the steel surface of the lake.

'I'm gonna bury 'im,' Mikey said. 'I'll take 'im down into the woods on the far side.'

'Want me to help you?' John said.

'No,' Mikey said. 'Anyhow, I gotta do it now. We ain't

gonna have time in the morning.'

Mikey slung Sean's body over his horse and led him down into the woods. He was gone for a long time.

With Mikey away, John continued to watch the woods. After a while, a pinprick of light appeared amidst the trees at the bottom of the slope. It grew brighter as John watched. Someone had lit a fire.

John imagined Hannah sitting by the fireside at home with her pipe in her hand and her Bible open on her lap. She was trying to teach William how to read from it, but William preferred to listen to her reading him stories aloud. His favourite was Jonah. He used to beg John to tell him what the sea was like. John would describe the smell of salt in the air, the hard Atlantic spray and the gulls wheeling over the Brooklyn waterfront. They would sit round their Minnesota fireside while John imagined for them a great fish, big enough to swallow a man, swimming on the tide right into New York harbour alongside the ships from Europe.

He heard Mikey crashing carelessly through the undergrowth on his way back up. He slumped down beside John, exhausted.

'Did the best I could,' he said. 'It weren't no deep grave since I didn't have no shovel, just my knife an' my hands.'

John looked in his saddle-bag for hard tack biscuits for them. Mikey noticed the fire, way down the slope right away.

'They must reckon we've crossed over the ridge towards Reckless. They think we're on the other side an' we can't see it,' he said. 'This is a gift. We'll rest up a few hours, then we'll sneak back down there and surprise 'em before daylight.'

'I dunno,' John said. 'This ain't what I came to do.'

51

Mikey spat. 'You're in this just as deep as I am. If you don't get 'em first, they sure as hell gonna get you.'

John considered.

'I offered to split that bank money with you. You don't wanna take it, that's down to you.'

'I ain't no bank-robber.'

'Look, no one knows you was in that robbery,' Mikey reasoned. 'There ain't no bounty on your head. They start chasin' you tomorrow in the daylight, or if we have to face 'em in Reckless, then they'll be able to work out who you are. Even if you don't get shot, someone's gonna describe you to someone and they'll work out that you wasn't at home on the farm when that bank in Calamity was took. You best deal with 'em while it's dark.'

John stared out into the night. The speck of firelight flickered, tempting him.

'What we gotta do first,' Mikey continued, 'is rest up. Then we'll get down there and kill 'em before dawn.'

5

A lone rider approached the farmhouse. He rode slowly, appraising everything he saw. He cast a critical eye over the worn gates, the repaired fences, the untidy verges and noted the poor condition of the stooks in the field. The place looked on the verge of bankruptcy. He paused to take in the view of the cabin up ahead. That still looked solid enough. The porch rail had been recently fixed; the yard in front of the house was swept and neat. The chicken huts were in fair condition and there was a goat tethered to a stake under a live oak.

The man reined in his horse a few yards short of the house but didn't dismount. He took off his hat and called out. He had steel-grey hair and was clean shaven with a heavy grey moustache. His face was tanned and lined from days spent on the trail. His buckskin jacket was worn and dusty. He called out again.

'Anybody there?'

Hannah appeared on the porch holding the shotgun ready to fire.

'What do you want?' she said. 'You know you ain't welcome here.'

The man started to dismount. Hannah waved the shotgun.

'You stay on that horse and turn right around.'

'I came to ask you somethin',' the man said. 'At least let me do that.'

'Why should I?' Hannah continued to hold the shotgun. 'You left here once. You can do it again. Right now.'

'Hannah, please. Let me see the boy.'

'He ain't here. He's out seein' to the traps.'

'Farm's lookin' fine,' he said. 'You're takin' good care of it.'

Hannah lowered the shotgun.

'We're takin' care of it. It ain't takin' care of us. It's mighty hard times out here in Wilderness, Lincoln.'

'The old house still standin' though. We sure did a good job on the cabin, didn't we?' Lincoln smiled. 'Remember how we was livin' in a tent all summer while we built it?'

Hannah began to smile then stopped herself.

'I'm done with rememberin',' she said. 'Now you just turn your horse around and ride on back to where you come from.'

'I want the boy to spend some time with me,' Lincoln said. 'There's things I can teach him. I asked the colonel an' I got permission for him to live at the fort, so long as I'm there.'

'You think I'm gonna agree to that?' Hannah said. 'He's fine here. There ain't nothing you can teach him at that fort that he can't learn here. You want him to be an army scout like you, livin' with soldiers, fightin' in the Indian wars.'

'No one's fightin' now,' Lincoln reasoned. 'I'd just teach 'im how to follow a trail, huntin', things he's gonna need.'

'When he's older, he'll make the choice himself,'

Hannah said. 'For now, I'm teaching him to read and we're teaching him farm life.'

'Well, the farming life ain't going so good, as far as I can see. What can your New York boy teach him about that anyways?'

Hannah raised the shotgun again.

'You speak about him, you speak respectful. John's a good man. He cares for us. William's got a home here.'

'You takin' up with a fella practically young enough to be your own,' Lincoln sneered.

'He stays here with us, he don't go off tryin' to live some frontier dream. A few years don't mean nothin' against that.'

Lincoln laughed. 'He ain't here now, that's for sure.'

'How d'you know that?'

'I seed 'im in Calamity.'

'Sure,' Hannah said. 'He's gone with his friends from the army to try an' get some money for us. There's a bounty their chasin'.'

'Well, he got some money for you all right. But it ain't no bounty. Not unless you count bank-robbin' as bounty.'

'What?'

'I seed 'im plain as day. The three of 'em robbed the Calamity bank yesterday mornin'. Then they hightailed it south towards Pearl Mountain.'

'You're lyin'.'

'This is the truth, I swear. I seed 'em with my own eyes. I recognized your New York boy right off. Never seen the other two before. The sheriff got up a posse and headed down to one of the short-cut passes, aiming to wait for 'em at Paradise Lake.'

'You're a liar, Lincoln. John ain't got a dishonest bone in his body.'

'Dunno whether they caught up with 'em. The posse ain't come back yet,' Lincoln continued. 'You don't believe me, Hannah, you ride into Calamity and see if I ain't tellin' the truth. The whole town is waitin' for that posse to come back.'

Hannah waved the shotgun.

'You get outa here right now. I ain't going to Calamity, or no place.'

'All right,' Lincoln said. 'William ain't here, so I'll go now. Just you remember, no one in Calamity knows your New York boy. Only me. I've only got to identify him to the sheriff an' there'll be a bounty on his head. He won't be able to come back here no more.'

Lincoln tugged at the reins and wheeled his horse around. Hannah kept the shotgun trained on him.

'Just you think on that, Hannah,' Lincoln called out to her. 'You think on letting William come to the fort. If the sheriff puts a bounty on your boy's head, I might hunt him myself. At least I know where to come lookin'.'

Lincoln urged his horse on. Hannah watched him leave before returning to the house.

Inside, Hannah decided to kill a chicken and boil it ready for William's return. It was his favourite and it would be a surprise. She loved to please him. She tried to dismiss what Lincoln had said from her mind, but she could not. He had seemed so certain. He had said the bank was robbed yesterday morning. That would be about the time when John and the others would have arrived in Calamity.

Hannah built up the fire, then she went outside to where the chickens were pecking in the dirt. She chose one of the poor layers, grabbed it and snapped its neck. She took it back to the porch and plucked out handfuls of feathers and stuffed them in a sack ready to be used for pillows.

Mikey could have robbed the bank, she thought. Maybe he had forced John to do it.

Maybe he had a gun on him. Maybe there was something from the army days that John hadn't told her. She fretted like this while she plucked and gutted the bird, unable to come to a conclusion. Part of her wanted to ride into Calamity to see if what he said was true; part of her wanted not to think of it at all.

William returned just as it was getting dark. The traps had been empty. He was tired and in a sour mood.

'I cooked a chicken for you,' Hannah said. 'It's your favourite.'

'You shouldn'ta done that, Ma,' he said. 'We ain't got enough to last the winter if we start killing 'em now.'

Hannah ignored his criticism.

'William,' she said, 'did you hear John and those men talking before they left, about what they might do in Calamity?'

'Yeah. They was gonna buy supplies. There wasn't enough here for them to take. Why?' William looked at her curiously.

'Oh, nothin'. I was just wondering.'

He laughed. 'What is there to do in Calamity?'

John followed Mikey close through the undergrowth. Even though they trod as lightly as they could, it seemed to him that their footsteps could be heard miles off. It was pitch black under the trees. John held his arms outstretched to protect his face against the branches. He heard Mikey cursing under his breath as he stumbled over roots and the uneven ground. Every now and then, over Mikey's shoulder,

John caught a glimpse of the fire up ahead.

The fire was at the centre of a small clearing. It had been recently built up and orange flames leapt two feet into the air. A neat pile of brushwood was stacked beside it a few feet away. Four men were sleeping under their blankets. Their faces were covered by their hats. Mikey and John stood still outside the ring of firelight in the darkness of the trees. They watched, trying to see if there was a guard.

'Mikey,' John grabbed Mikey's arm. His stomach lurched at the horror of what he was about to do.

Mikey shook his arm free. 'Just watch my back,' he hissed.

John drew his gun and trod in Mikey's footsteps towards the sleeping men.

Mikey stopped again.

'On three,' he whispered. 'One, two—'

Mikey leapt forward into the ring of firelight, Colt in hand, blasting from the hip. There was no movement from the sleeping men. Mikey drilled them all. John was just about to follow him, when he realized.

'It's a trap, Mikey,' he yelled.

Mikey stooped and pulled at one of the blankets. There were only branches and piles of leaves underneath. He looked up at John in disbelief. From the shadows on the other side of the camping ground, they heard weapons being cocked.

'Run,' Mikey yelled.

John turned and plunged back into the darkness. Mikey was behind him. Bullets tore through the trees. Men's voices were shouting. John sprang forward into the under-growth. Branches whipped his face. Thorns tore his clothes. Another volley of shots screamed around him. His lungs were bursting. He felt sick with fear and the agony of running.

He ran on, his gun in his hand, holding up his arm to try to protect his face. All he could hear were his own crashing footsteps and the blood pounding in his head. His mouth was dry. There were more shots. Bullets spat through the trees.

He was climbing now. He must be approaching the ridge. The shouts of the men, calling out to each other in the darkness, sounded further away. The first streaks of grey light showed through the high branches. John stopped, gulping air to catch his breath; his heart smashed against his ribs. He turned and listened. Mikey wasn't behind him. He strained to hear the sound of running. The sound of footsteps. There was nothing.

John holstered his gun, sat down and leaned against a tree. He waited for his breathing to return to normal and his heart to stop pounding. He could make out the firelight dancing in the trees way below him. The men were still calling to each other, but they weren't getting nearer. He had to go back.

Treading carefully again, John picked his way through the brush. He paused and listened after every step. The men seemed to have given up the chase and returned to the fire. He couldn't be sure how many there were. Every few yards he whispered Mikey's name. No answer.

A few yards outside the ring of firelight, John stopped. He watched the men sitting round, having clearly given up the chase, unwilling to come after them in the pitch-dark woods. Oné of the men said something, heaved himself to his feet and walked out of the light straight towards him. John froze. At the edge of the firelight, the man tripped on something. He cursed and took another step. Then he let out a shout.

'Hey, we got one of 'em right here.'

The man hauled something back into the firelight: it was Mikey's body. The others clustered round.

'Look at that,' the man said. 'Sonofabitch got a bullet hole in 'im.' His voice shook with excitement. 'We got 'im and we never even knowed it. That was some pretty fine shootin' there, boys.'

'He still breathin?' asked one of the others.

The man felt for a pulse.

'Just,' he said. 'But he won't be for long, I reckon. Damn. If that reward poster said dead or alive, we could finish 'im off right now an' still claim the money.'

'He ain't gonna make it as far as Calamity anyways.'

'Well, at least we got one of 'em,' another man said. 'The other two are still out there somewheres.' He stared out at the darkness.

'Think they'll come for us again?'

The first man laughed. 'They took the bait once. They ain't gonna do it again.'

He kicked Mikey's body.

'You all see the way this 'un tried to shoot us when he thought we were sleepin'?'

He turned to the others.

'Somebody bring some coffee with 'em? Sure could use a cup.'

John trod carefully away from the firelight. The men were boasting about what they would like do to Mikey.

Dawn was showing like a smear of blood when John reached the ridge. The horses were tethered to a red maple. John took a swig of water from his canteen. After a moment's reflection, he exchanged Mikey's saddle-bag, stamped with the initials MD and which contained the money from the robbery, with his own. He untied Mikey and Sean's horses and sent them off into the woods, then mounted up and started over the ridge and down towards the plain. Reckless was a two-day ride.

6

Reckless was a farm town. Two rows of wooden buildings faced each other along a dirt street. Most of them were single storey. A few supported an upper floor with a balcony. Stores carried goods to tempt the farmers: dry goods, clothing, cigars and liquor, hardware. Then there was a saloon and a bank. Supplies were brought up by wagon from Kansas.

John left his horse in the livery stable and headed up the street to the saloon. As he approached, the swing doors burst open and a man was flung out. He landed on his back in the dirt. His face creased in pain as he hauled himself to his feet. The saloon keeper appeared in the doorway with a shotgun in his hands.

'I didn't mean nothin' by it, I swear,' the man protested.

The saloon keeper lifted the barrel of the shotgun. The man held out his hands to defend himself and ran off down the street. When he was satisfied that the man was a good distance away, the saloon keeper lowered the shotgun and stepped back inside. John hesitated for a moment and then followed him in.

The saloon was empty apart from a woman who sat at a

table laying out a hand of patience. The saloon keeper ignored John and started polishing a large, oak-framed mirror which hung behind the bar.

'What kin I getcha?' he said eventually, still working on the mirror.

'I was wonderin' if you had a room to rent.'

The woman put down her cards and looked at John.

'Ground don't get no softer as you get older. Sure could use a good night's sleep.'

'We got a room,' the saloon keeper said. 'Where are you from?'

'Wilderness County,' John said. 'North of Pearl.'

'Cattleman?' the saloon keeper enquired idly.

'Nope. Lookin' for someone. Heard he might be passin' through here. Knowed 'im from the war.'

The man stiffened. 'You with the Yankees?'

'I was,' John said. 'Ain't with no one now, though,' he added cautiously.

In the mirror, John saw that the woman was watching him.

'I'm from Missouri,' the saloon keeper said.

'Well,' John said, 'war mixed the whole country up, so far as I can see.'

'I was took prisoner. I spent most of it locked up in a tobacco warehouse in Delaware,' the barkeep continued. 'Yankees didn't kill us on the battlefield, so they tried to starve us to death instead. Some weeks, only rations we got was rat meat.'

'Everyone of us ate rat, some time or other,' John said.

'I seen men ask the guards to shoot 'em. Men who was locked up for a year or more. Never saw daylight. Never hardly got fed. They would walk straight up to the guards and beg 'em. I seen them Yankee guards bayonet men to death just for askin', an' laugh while they done it. They was cruel sonsabitches.'

The man picked up his cotton rag and started polishing the mirror again.

'You ever see somethin' like that?'

'Can't say I have,' John said. 'An' I'm glad of it.'

'I used to think,' the saloon keeper continued, 'what I'd do if I came across one o' them guards as did that.'

John waited for him to go on.

'One o' them Yankee boys who stuck a man right through with 'is bayonet, just cos he asked 'im to.' The man shook his head with disbelief. All the time he continued polishing the mirror.

The woman was watching him.

'Thomas,' she said quietly, 'you ain't gived this man a drink. He's waitin' on you.'

'I'm busy,' he said. 'You get 'im a drink.'

The woman sighed and got up from her cards. She walked behind the bar and poured John a whiskey.

'Name's Grace. This here's Thomas. Whiskey's the only drink we got,' she explained. 'Beer's run dry. New mash ain't ready yet.'

'Ask 'im the question,' Thomas said, still concentrating on his polishing.

Grace sighed again. She had asked the question a hundred times.

'He wants to know what he should do if he runs into one o' them Yankee prison-camp guards. He asks everyone who comes in the same question.'

Thomas seemed to see specks of dirt on the mirror that no-one else could and polished hard.

'Anyone who gets the answer wrong, he throws 'em out,' Grace explained.

'Many get thrown out?' John asked.

'Yeah, some days,' Grace said. 'The answer changes, so it's hard to tell.'

Thomas stopped polishing. He glared at John. 'Well?'

'It's a good question,' John said. 'I'm still thinking on it.'

Thomas laughed to himself.

'That fella left just as I was comin' in, did he get the answer wrong?'

'Sure did,' Grace said. 'He said the war was over.'

'Damn fool answer,' Thomas sneered and turned back to the mirror. 'Everyone knows that.' John could see he was smiling.

Grace returned to her cards. Thomas carried on inspecting his mirror. John took a seat at one of the empty tables and nursed his whiskey.

A while later, a soldier in full uniform rode up and dismounted outside. He strode in to the saloon, touched his hat to Grace and stepped up to the bar. The soldier was young and his uniform was new. There was an awkward moment while he waited, expecting Thomas to speak to him.

Grace said, 'You know we don't serve no soldiers in here. What d'you want?'

Thomas turned to face him.

'I got a message.'

The soldier didn't know whether to speak to Thomas or Grace and looked anxiously from one to the other.

'It's from Colonel Pride at Fort Trenton. It's for the sheriff. It's for all o' you. For the whole town, but the sheriff ain't in his office so I come in here.'

65

'It's a Tuesday afternoon,' Grace said. 'Sheriff ain't never in his office on a Tuesday afternoon.'

'You know where I could find him, ma'am?' the soldier said.

Thomas clenched the edge of the bar until his knuckles became white.

'I surely do,' Grace continued. 'But it's more that the sheriff don't wanna be found. He's upstairs makin' friends, if you get my meanin'.'

'Were you in the war, boy?' Thomas broke in. His voice was hard as glass.

'N-no, sir.'

'Leave 'im be, Thomas,' Grace said. 'He ain't nothin' but a kid.'

'He gotta answer,' Thomas said. He reached down and brought out his shotgun. He laid it on the bar between him and the soldier. The soldier took a pace backwards.

'Sir, I gotta deliver Colonel Pride's message,' he spoke quickly, keeping his eyes on the shotgun. 'Sir, Colonel Pride sends his compliments and says the fort is expecting an Indian attack. A band of Lakota Sioux are in the area. They think the peace agreement that Fighting Eagle signed cheated them outa their land.'

'It sure didn't give 'em no land, did it?' Grace said. 'Your colonel expects them to obey orders an' run off back to the rservation when they're told to, like they're soldier boys in his precious regiment, does he?'

'Pardon me, ma'am. The colonel says it ain't safe for no one to leave town. He says everyone gotta stay here until he tells 'em different. He's gonna send a detachment across to act as protection for the townsfolk. There's a group of wagons heading west outa Kansas and he's gonna have us escort them up here, so they can stay in town until all this is blowed over.'

'Put that shotgun away, Thomas,' Grace said. 'The boy's just followin' his orders.'

'Yes, ma'am. Thank you, ma'am. That's what I'm doin'.'

'All right,' Grace said. 'That's enough with the "yes ma'ams". This colonel o' yours,' she continued, 'he a good man?'

'Why, yes, he is, ma'am.' The soldier seemed surprised at the question. 'Every man in the regiment would say so.'

'He sign the agreement with Fighting Eagle?'

'Yes, he did. I was part of the detachment that accompanied him, ma'am. I was proud to.'

Grace reflected. 'Seems to me like the Sioux got a fight with the army an' if the army come into the town then the Sioux are gonna follow 'em. If the army stay in the fort or out on the plains, the Sioux ain't gonna come near the town. Looks like the army is bringin' us trouble.'

'Colonel Pride will be sendin' a detachment as protection,' the soldier repeated. 'An' a detachment to escort the wagons from Kansas.'

'Let me ask you somethin',' Thomas said.

The soldier seemed relieved not to have to hear more of Grace's criticism of his colonel. He turned to Thomas. His eyes fell on the shotgun which still lay on the bar.

'You ever hear a man ask a Yankee soldier to shoot 'im?'

'Thomas,' Grace said, warning.

'Can't say I have, sir. That would be the damnedest thing.'

Thomas picked up the shotgun.

'It's time you was leavin',' Grace said. 'We'll give the colonel's message to the sheriff soon as he gets his britches back on.'

Thomas waved the shotgun.

'That's the wrong answer, soldier boy.'

He stepped round from behind the bar and swung the shotgun high ready to crack the soldier on the side of the head. The boy flinched. John leapt up and grabbed the gun. Both barrels loosed off into the ceiling. There was a shout and a scream from upstairs. Grace jumped to her feet, scattering cards everywhere. She yelled at the soldier to scat. John tussled for the shotgun, eventually wrenching it away from Thomas. The soldier dashed out into the street.

There was the pounding of someone running downstairs. The sheriff burst through the door at the foot of the stairs. He was red-faced; a short, big-bellied man wearing long johns and a hat. He waved a Colt .45.

'Damnit to hell, Thomas. It's my Tuesday afternoon. Can't you leave off for one day?'

John placed the shotgun back on the bar.

'Colonel Pride sent you a message, Sheriff,' Grace said, stooping down to pick up the cards. 'Sioux are on the warpath. Looks like trouble.'

7

John was woken by the sound of a .45 being cocked. He opened his eyes to see the sheriff and Thomas, the saloon keeper, at the end of his bed leering down at him. They both had guns trained on him.

'Got 'im, ain't we, Thomas?'

'Yessir. Sure have.' Thomas had a crazy, lopsided grin across his face.

The attic room above the saloon bar was small. There wasn't much room for anything apart from the brass bed. The saddle-bags were on the floor beside the bed and John's gunbelt lay on top of them. An open window overlooked the street. From outside, came the creak of wagons and the sound of horses' hoofs and men's voices.

'Now,' the sheriff said, 'we're gonna do this nice an' slow. You should 'preciate that, seein' as how you just woke up, Mr Donnal.'

Thomas gave a short laugh which sounded like the whinny of a horse.

'Thomas here is gonna pick up your gun an' those bags o' yours, since you ain't gonna be needin 'em. Soon as he's done that, you're gonna get your pants back on an' come with us.'

'What did you call me?' John said.

'Shaddup.' The sheriff's face hardened. 'I ain't said nothin' about you talkin'.'

'I'm just sayin' . . .' John protested.

The sheriff raised his gun and pointed it directly at John's eyes. A small vein throbbed at the side of the sheriff's head.

'You don't say nothin',' he breathed, 'till I say you can.'

Thomas grabbed the gunbelt and the saddle-bags.

'Saddle-bags sure is heavy, Sheriff,' he grinned.

'You keep 'im covered good, Thomas.'

John levered himself out of bed and pulled on his pants and shirt. Each movement was followed by a wave of Thomas' Colt. Thomas led the way downstairs, John followed and the sheriff came behind with his gun trained on John's back. In the saloon, Grace sat at a table with her patience hand laid out. A younger woman, in a grey cotton dress and a long apron, sat beside her watching the game.

'Why, mornin', Sheriff,' Grace said, affecting surprise. 'It ain't Tuesday no more. What are you doin' here?'

'I'm carryin' out my civic duty. I'm arrestin' this man who is a criminal with a bounty on his head.'

'What're you talkin' about, Sheriff? Thomas ain't got no bounty on his head. He just had experiences in the war made 'im like he is.'

Colour rose in the sheriff's face.

'This ain't no jokin' matter, Gracie,' the sheriff blustered. 'This ain't woman's work neither.'

'I know what kinda woman's work you like, Sheriff,' the girl said innocently. ' 'Specially on a Tuesday afternoon.'

'N-now you shut up about that, Charity,' the sheriff stammered. He turned to Thomas. 'Get on, Thomas. We gotta git 'im over to the cells and lock 'im up.'

A line of wagons and ox carts had drawn up along the street. The army escort was still mounted up beside them. This was the wagon train which should have been heading west out of Kansas. A sergeant called the order for the troopers to dismount. More orders were shouted and the soldiers led their horses to an assembly point up the street.

Men and women climbed down from their wagons. They were thin-faced, determined people, used to hardship. They confronted this setback with weary stoicism, knowing that their promised land still lay ahead of them. Having gathered their ragged children and all their possessions into the wagons, nothing was going to stop them now.

They watched Thomas lead the way out of the saloon with the saddle-bags and gunbelt over his shoulder. They saw the town sheriff with his gun at John's back escorting a prisoner to jail. John saw contempt for him in their eyes. As the three men climbed the steps to the sheriff's office, John turned to the him again.

'Look, I can explain—' he began.

With the people from the wagon train as an audience, the sheriff cracked his gun across the side of John's head. John reeled.

'I tol' you to keep your mouth shut,' he shouted. 'There's decent folks here. They don' wanna hear your whinin' excuses.' He turned to see whether people had been watching, hoping they had. Grace and Charity were standing in the doorway of the saloon. They seemed to be sharing a private joke.

Inside the office, the sheriff cracked John over the head again with the side of his pistol. John's head rang and blood ran down his neck. John was kicked across the small office and into the cell. Thomas threw down the gunbelt and saddle-bags on the office desk, then kicked John's feet away from under him. John crashed down on to the floor. Thomas lit into him, kicking him in the back and ribs while the sheriff watched. Eventually, John lay still. The sheriff pulled Thomas away and locked the cell door.

'Got us a bank-robber, Thomas. Ain't never had one in Reckless before.'

He hung the saddle-bags and John's gunbelt on a hook on the wall and sat down at his desk, grinning to himself. He reached into his desk drawer and brought out a wooden cigar box.

'Tell you what, I'm minded to light up an ol' stogie, even if it is early in the day.' He struck a match and a wreath of rich, blue smoke coiled around him. He leaned back in his chair and put his feet on the desk.

'I ain't gonna offer you one, Thomas, because these are my favourite. Tell you what though,' he added, 'you keep this up an' I'm thinkin' I may offer you the position of honorary deputy.'

'Why, thank you kindly, Sheriff,' Thomas beamed. 'I sure would like that. How d'you know it was him, Sheriff?'

'Colonel Pride's lieutenant said the army got word that there had bin a robbery up at Calamity. Posse followed 'em as far as Paradise Lake. They got one. The other two got away.' The sheriff puffed contentedly on his cigar. 'I remembered seein' this fella in the saloon yesterday. Remembered he had a fat saddle-bag alongside his chair. When the lieutenant told me this morning, I put two an' two together. That saddle-bag's fulla bank dollars, I'll betcha.'

He pushed himself to his feet and undid the flap of the bag. The initials M.D. were burnt into the leather. The top of the canvas money bag showed.

'See?'

'Damn, if it ain't,' Thomas said.

'Now don't you go tellin' no one about the money, or I won't be able to make you a deputy. You understand, now, Thomas? With the wagon train in town we don't want that kinda information gettin' about.'

Thomas agreed quickly.

'What you can tell folks is, I arrested Mikey Donnal, leader of the Donnal Twins, right here in Reckless this mornin'.'

'An' I helped you,' Thomas added proudly.

'You sure did.'

'I'll tell you one more thing too. Know how I know the fella's name, even though I never set eyes on 'im before?'

The sheriff didn't pause for Thomas to answer. He merely pointed to the initials on the saddle-bags. The sheriff leaned back in his chair again and took another satisfied puff on his stogie.

Hours later, John woke. His body was aching and bruised and he had a raging thirst. There was no one in the office. He could see his gunbelt and the saddle-bag hanging on the opposite wall. The flap which had held the bank bag was undone and the money was gone.

There was a small barred window in the back wall of the cell. John stood on the wooden bed to look out. The window looked south. There was nothing to see but miles of grassland and a hard, blue sky.

John thought of Hannah and their cabin in Wilderness. He pictured her delight when he came home with a deer he had shot in the woods, or how she would be looking out for him when he returned from the fields. He remembered the tender look in her eyes and the gentle way she spoke.

Then he remembered the parched ground in the barley field, the times the traps had been empty, running out of hay for the horses and not being able to afford to buy more. He remembered William's angry face, blaming him because he had failed to provide for them, all the time comparing him to his real father – the man who had left when he was a baby and whom he hardly knew.

John gripped the bars to the cell with both fists. Rage boiled within him: anger against Mikey for leading him into trouble; fury at the men who had shot Sean in the back; contempt for the sheriff who had stolen the money.

John knew what he had to do. He had to get the money back and hand it in. He had to find the Preacher and claim the bounty. He had to get home to the farm with enough dollars to see them through the winter. Then, maybe, they would be able to survive the year ahead. He rested his head against the cell bars, stared at the stone floor and waited for the sheriff to return.

'Your father's been here,' Hannah said.

She held William gently by the shoulders and looked straight into his eyes. At first, the boy thought she was talking about John.

'He's back already?' William was pleased.

'No. Your natural father. He came by.'

'Oh,' William said, not knowing what this meant.

'He wants you to go and live with him.'

William looked at her.

'For a while, anyway. He's an army scout and they've posted him to Fort Trenton. There's trouble with a band of Sioux down around Reckless.'

'I dunno, Ma.'

They had talked about this often. William had wanted it. Now he was nervous.

'You don't have to answer now,' Hannah said. 'You don't have to answer at all, if you don't want to. I'm just tellin' you what he said. You can think on it and then we can talk about it some more.'

William looked into her face for guidance. She smiled at him and ruffled his hair.

'Anyhow,' she went on. 'He said he saw John in Calamity and there was some sort of trouble.'

'What kinda trouble, Ma? John's real careful. He don't get into trouble.' Hannah heard the anxiety rise in his voice.

'I'm going into Calamity to find out. I want you to saddle up Runaway for me.'

'But you don't never go into Calamity, Ma.'

'I know. I'll talk to Mr Morgan at the store. He'll know what's going on.'

'Let me go, Ma. I don't want those men bein' mean to you.'

'No. I want to go myself this time, William. I'll just talk to Mr Morgan. He's a good man. I won't talk to no one else. Anyhow, you got to keep an eye on those traps.' She smiled at him. 'You keep bringin' in the pelts the way you are, we might have enough to sell. It's important work you're doin', William.'

William could see his mother's mind was made up. He went out to the barn to saddle the horse for her.

Even though the cell bench was hard, John slept most of the afternoon. No one came into the sheriff's office. He woke with thirst still clawing at this throat and lay listening to the sounds from the street outside. The men from the wagon train were unhitching their animals and leading them up the street to the livery stable. Men and women's voices were audible as they passed by the office door. An army sergeant shouted commands somewhere off in the distance. Shadows from the bars on the cell window lay across John's body.

Suddenly, he heard a familiar sound. Something he hadn't heard for years. But there it was, clear and unmistakable over the noise of the wagons. The light, melodic chimes of an expensive pocket watch drifted on the afternoon air. They were just as pretty as John remembered them.

Then he recalled the last time he had heard them. He saw the gloating face of the Andersonville guard laughing down at him from the pigeon coop, holding the watch in full view for John to see as the sweet tune played.

Almost as soon as it had started, the chiming ceased. For a moment, John doubted what he had heard. He stood on the bench again and stared out of the cell window. There was no one. Just the miles of grassy plain in the failing afternoon sun. The sound must have come from the street. The Preacher must be in town.

The door to the sheriff's office opened. Charity, from the saloon, stood in the doorway with a hunk of bread in one hand and a bottle of water in the other.

'They sent me across with these,' she said. She pushed the food and water through the bars to John. 'My,' she said, catching sight of John's face. 'They sure gived you a beatin'.'

John drank quickly from the bottle. Charity leaned back

on the sheriff s desk. 'You really a bank robber?'

'No,' John said.

'I thought not. I said so to Gracie. You kin always tell if a man's mean by his eyes. You ain't got mean eyes at all.' She laughed lightly. 'You got real nice eyes.'

'Thank you, ma'am.' John smiled at her.

His politeness encouraged the girl to go on.

'Not like the sheriff. He's got hog eyes, 'specially when he's bin drinkin'.' She reflected. 'And Thomas, well, he's got crazy eyes. They roll aroun' sometimes like they're gonna pop right outa his head.'

'Sounds like you made a study of it,' John said.

'Well, I guess I have. I just know you can tell a lot about a person by his eyes. I got nice eyes too. An' Gracie, she's got real nice eyes. Real greeny-blue an' calm. I love to look in Gracie's eyes.'

John tore a hunk off the loaf and chewed it.

'Good bread,' he said. 'Thanks. You make this?'

Charity laughed again.

'I like cookin',' she explained. 'But I ain't no good at it. Thomas won't let me do cookin' no more at the saloon. He says I burn everythin'. Says I gotta stick to whorin'.' She pulled a face. 'Don't reckon I'm much good at that neither. Leastways, nobody never says I'm good at it.' Charity sighed. 'Guess I ain't much good at nothin'.'

'You're good at talkin',' John ventured.

A beaming smile lit Charity's face.

'Why, thank you, mister. Yes, I guess I am good at talkin'. I like to talk. An' I like talkin' to Gracie best of all.'

The street door opened suddenly. The sheriff stood there. He saw Charity and his face fell.

'What are you doin' here?'

'I just brought some bread an' water over. Thomas tol' me to.'

'Sounds like you was yackin' to me,' said the sheriff. 'You ain't got nothing worth sayin'.' He nodded towards the door. 'Now, go on. Get.'

Charity avoided the sheriff's eye and slipped out of the door.

The sheriff sat down at his desk and looked across at John.

'I just bin havin' a conversation about you,' he said.

'Yeah?'

'There's a fella from the fort comin' to take you into army custody. I'm handin' you over to Colonel Pride.' The sheriff chuckled. 'He's a busy man. He don't believe in no long trials with lawyers and such. He'll string you up soon as look at you.'

'I told you,' John said. 'You got the wrong man.'

'Try tellin' that to the colonel.'

'I ain't Donnal. I told you,' John insisted.

'Another thing,' the sheriff added, ignoring him. 'The colonel's gonna want to know what you done with the money. I already tol' him those saddle-bags with your initials stamped on 'em was empty when I arrested you.'

John was silent.

'You're gonna say you ain't Donnal an' that the sheriff stole the money. That's what every no-good varmint says. Before you go wastin' your breath denyin' everythin', just think on who the colonel's gonna believe. Some bank-robbin' low life or the sheriff o' Reckless? Coupla days, an' you're gonna be decoratin' the hangin' tree.' He turned away from John and reached in the desk drawer for his box of stogies.

'Anyhow, I ain't minded to sit here listenin' to you lyin'

about who you ain't. When this fella comes, I'll be across the street in the saloon.'

8

'Why, Hannah,' old man Morgan greeted her on the porch to the general store, 'we ain't seen you in town for months.'

Morgan put down the broom he had been sweeping with and followed Hannah inside. A bell tinkled as he opened the door. The store smelled of roasting coffee beans and carried the scent of fruit and the bunches of herbs which hung above the counter. Morgan turned to the stove.

'Let me pour you a cup of coffee. You've had a long ride.'

He set a wooden chair for her beside the counter and poured two cups of coffee. A flitch of bacon was set on a marble slab on the counter. A jar of candy twists stood beside it. Sacks of white beans were open on the floor with their tops folded back. There was a pile of sacks of flour and bags of sugar. A box of apples was by the door. Morgan was genuinely pleased to see Hannah.

'You'll be wantin' your usual flour an' beans, I expect. We got some good coffee in too. Real nice, rich taste to it. I bin recommending it to all my customers.' Morgan peered at her over the top of his spectacles. 'An' I hope you're lookin' after John real good. It's six months since he run that fella with a gun outa here. I ain't seen 'im since. I sure was grateful to 'im that day—'

'I ain't come to place an order,' Hannah interrupted him.

'Now, if it's credit, Hannah, I ain't so sure,' the old man blustered. 'I got people owin' me already. But maybe we kin work somethin' out. I know it's bin a harsh season.'

'No, Mr Morgan, it ain't that. Although we sure are runnin' outa supplies. I want to ask you about the robbery at the bank.'

Morgan looked at her curiously. 'Well.' He scratched his head. 'I can't think what you want to know about that for. One day last week two fellas burst into the bank just as it was openin' up, waving their guns in the air. They got away with two bags o' cash. Ran off round the corner. There was another one waitin' for them there with the horses.'

'One of them didn't hold up the bank?' queried Hannah.

'Well, one of 'em was waitin' with the horses, if that's what you mean. They'll catch 'em though. They know who they are.' Morgan chuckled to himself. 'They ain't so smart. There was a Wanted poster pinned up in the bank. Didn't have no picture on it, so one could recognize 'em, just their names. One of 'em spotted it and tore it down, yelled out to his friend, "Lookee here, we're famous".'

He looked at Hannah to see her reaction.

'Don't you see? He told everyone who they were,' Morgan went on, his eyes twinkling with amusement.

'What were their names?'

'The Five Points Twins, name of Donnal,' Morgan said. 'Can't tell you how they figure they're twins, seein' as how there's three of 'em.'

'Did they go after them?' Hannah said.

81

'Surely did,' old man Morgan said, enjoying the story. 'Young Johnson from the livery stable got shot at. They didn't hit him, but he was so scared he fell off the roof an' busted his arm. A few of the guys chased 'em. There was a lot o' shootin'. Some of them say one of them was hit, some of them say no one was. Then the deputies figured they were headed to Paradise Lake an' took the shortcut through the Baxter place.'

Hannah listened carefully.

'Shot one of 'em bad down there. The other two got away. Say, you all right, Hannah? You're lookin' kinda pale.'

Hannah cleared her throat and tried to smile.

'I'm fine.'

'Well, Sam Parsons, the deputy, told me the one they caught had a bullet in 'im. They thought he was dyin'. Anyhow, they left 'im while they went off the next day lookin' for the others. When they came back in the evenin', expectin' to find a corpse, he was gone. They couldn't find 'im nowhere. Sheriff raised merry hell about that. Blamed ol' Sam for leavin' him. Called 'im a boss-eyed ol' coot an' all kindsa names. Brung down curses on 'im an' everything. Soon as they got back to town, Sam said he wasn't standin' for no more o' that and quit being deputy right then an' there.'

Old Morgan laughed.

'I've knowed Sam Parsons twenty-five years. When he says he's gonna do somethin', he's sure gonna do it.'

The bell tinkled as the door opened.

A sharp-faced woman entered. Her hair was scraped back into a tight bun and she wore a black gown. She held a wicker basket over her arm.

'Mornin', Mrs Ford,' Morgan said cheerfully.

The woman recognized Hannah and froze. 'I'll come back later, if you're busy, Mr Morgan.'

'No, no. Come right in.'

Hannah stood up, avoiding the woman's gaze.

'I don't know as I wish to stand in line after a half-breed.' Mrs Ford's voice sounded like splintering glass.

'Now, there's no need for—' Morgan began.

'After what them savages did to my grandpappy, I don't understand you, Mr Morgan, I really don't. Letting one o' them in a perfectly fine store. . . .' She paused. 'And she's driven her husband out and has taken up with a man barely older than her own child, from what I heard.'

'Now, Mrs Ford—' Morgan tried to remonstrate with her.

'If there was another general store in this Godforsaken town, Mr Morgan,' Mrs Ford's voice was rising to a screech, 'I would be takin' my custom there.'

Hannah stood up and quickly walked out of the store.

As she was mounting her horse, Morgan ran out after her. He handed a two-pound bag of coffee beans up to her.

'Take this coffee, Hannah,' he said. 'You remember me to John and William now. I ain't seen John in I don't know how long.'

John jumped up as the door to the sheriff's office opened abruptly. A tall, square-built man stood in the doorway. Long, steel-grey hair flowed from under his hat. He was unshaven with a heavy grey moustache. He wore a pair of Navy Colts over his buckskin jacket. He stared hard at John for a moment and then acknowledged him with a brief nod.

'Where's the sheriff?'

'Over at the saloon.'

'Good.'

The man strode into the office and sat on the desk.

'Boy, somebody sure gived you a whuppin'.'

John sat back down on the cell bench. 'That what you come to tell me?' he said. 'Who are you anyways?'

The man considered. 'Well, my current employment is army scout attached to Colonel Pride's regiment out at Fort Trenton. My orders is to take you out to the fort where I believe the colonel aims to make you stand trial for robbin' the bank at Calamity. 'Course, when it comes to trials, the colonel is a very direct man. He gets straight to the hangin'. He don't bother much with no courtroom.'

'I told the sheriff he's got the wrong man,' John said. 'But he ain't listenin'.'

The scout looked at him. 'Seems to me you're fresh outa luck, friend.' Then he added, 'You don't know who I am, do ya?'

'I ain't never seen you before,' John said. 'How can I know you? What's your meanin' anyways?'

'Where's the money?'

'That what you're after? Was in them saddle-bags over there.' John indicated the empty bags hanging beside his gunbelt on the opposite wall. 'Look's like it ain't no more. I guess the sheriff took it. Good as told me he had. He knows no one's gonna believe me. 'Specially this colonel ain't.'

'You're right there. You ain't got a cat in hell's chance of him believing you.' He leaned forward. 'You're John Wright, ain't you?'

John sat up abruptly.

'How d'you know my name?'

The man looked hard at John. 'I ain't sure you'll want to hear this. But I want you to do something for me. We might be able to strike a deal an' help each other out.'

John listened.

'I'm Hannah's husband,' the man said simply.

'What?' John said. 'What's happened to her?' He felt winded. Fear clawed within him.

'Ain't nothin' happened,' the man reassured him. 'I'm just explainin' who I am. Name's Lincoln.'

'I know your name,' John said. 'Everyone up in Wilderness knows about you.'

'That's cos my family was the first settlers up in that part of the country. My grandpa and grandma arrived in a covered wagon with a bunch o' traps, a bottle o' red eye an' the clothes they stood up in. They made friends with the Sioux right off.'

'I heard that too.'

'Anyhow, later on, I met up with Hannah. William was comin' an' we built that cabin. Set ourselves up on that farm. I was young. Found a travelling preacher who would marry us an' we got proper church married. Folks kin take against a person who's got Indian blood. I did it to protect her.'

'I ain't interested in you an' Hannah, mister. What's done is done,' John said.

'I weren't cut out for the life of a sodbuster,' Lincoln continued. 'The open range is in my blood, same as my pappy an' grandpappy. Anyhow, that's more or less how come I'm a scout for the army right now.'

'Mister—'

Lincoln pulled himself up. 'I want William to spend some time with me. He's got my blood in him. I want him to come and stay out at the fort so I kin teach him the frontier life.'

'An' if I agree, you're gonna spring me from this jail-house. Is that it?' John snapped. 'You know I can't agree to that. That's William's choice.'

Lincoln hesitated. He studied John's face for a moment.

'You're a good man. I kin see why Hannah picked you. That ain't what I'm askin'. I just want you to let the boy think it out for himself an' not stand in the way o' his doin' that.'

'Mister, stuck in here, I can't let nobody think out nothin'.'

Lincoln stood up and took the cell keys off the peg on the wall.

'I'm gonna let you out. You gotta slug me hard so's I get a nice, peachy bruise comin'. Then you lock me in the cell an' you kin' take off. I'll tell the sheriff you jumped me.'

'He ain't gonna believe that,' John said.

'He kin believe what he likes,' Lincoln said briefly. 'My word against his.' He put his guns on the sheriff's desk and unlocked the cell door.

'What are you gonna do now?' Lincoln asked.

'I gotta get that money back. If I don't hand it back to the Calamity bank, I ain't gonna be able to live up there no more. Then there's another piece o' business I gotta take care of.'

Lincoln nodded.

'Now when you slug me,' he grinned, 'make it on the left side. I got a tooth in there bin givin' me gyp. You might get rid of it for me.'

John buckled on his gunbelt and checked the chamber of his Colt.

'I just want ya to know, I appreciate your directness in what you bin tellin' me,' he said.

Before Lincoln could answer, John swung a mighty punch and caught him on the left side of the jaw. He heard the snap of breaking teeth and Lincoln's knees buckled. The big man went down. John grabbed him under the arms and hauled him into the cell and left him in a heap on the floor. He locked the door and tossed the keys across the office.

John opened the street door cautiously. There were a few people seeing to their wagons, but nobody noticed him. Charity was leaning against the wall of the saloon. She was crying. She noticed John and started to wave to him. Then she realized he didn't want to be seen and looked away.

Closing the door behind him, John stepped out into the street. He pulled his hat down low and walked quickly in the direction of the livery stables, keeping tight to the wall. He touched his hat to two women talking outside the store. They smiled politely. John felt safe enough. The townsfolk who didn't recognize him would think he was from the wagon train.

The horses were all in their stalls in the livery stables. They had been fed and watered. John found his own horse in an end stall. John patted her gently on the flank and whispered in her ear. He was relieved to see her. The horse was his only link with home. He heard footsteps rustle through the straw behind him. He turned quickly. It was Charity. A purple bruise was swelling her cheek, her lip was split and there was a line of dried blood at the corner of her mouth.

'I saw you come down here, so I followed you,' she burst out. 'You busted outa jail?'

'What's happened to you?' John said.

'Never mind that. I don't wanna talk about it.'

Charity seemed close to tears. Her hands were shaking. John sat her down in the straw, out of sight of the street. He knelt down beside her.

'Listen to me, Charity,' he said. 'You ain't seen me an' you don't know nothin' about me bein' outa jail. It's dangerous for you, you understand? The sheriff's gonna be awful mad.'

'I hate the sheriff,' Charity protested. 'He's mean. I ain't gonna say nothing to no one. Let me help you.'

John patted her on the head. 'I sure 'preciate the offer, Charity, but there ain't nothing you kin do for me.'

'Yes, there is,' Charity countered.

'Yeah?' John smiled at her.

'Yeah,' she said. 'I know where the sheriff hid the money.'

'What?'

Charity's eyes sparkled. 'See?' she said. 'Tol' you I could help you.'

'Where?' John said. 'Where did he hide it?'

'I'll tell you if you'll do somethin' for me.'

Charity picked up a handful of straw and let it fall through her fingers.

'Where are you goin' when you leave Reckless?' she continued.

'Home,' John said. 'Back to Wilderness County.'

Charity looked down at the straw, suddenly afraid to look him in the eye. 'Mister, if I tell you where the money is, will you take me with you?'

The girl's voice was plain and unaffected. Her question was simple and honest. All the pain which lay behind her request, the reasons why she had made it, was concealed.

'Charity,' John said gently, 'I gotta wife an' a son.'

88

'I only meant I could help with the chores. You wouldn't have to pay me or nothin'. I could jus' be there. I just wanna be in a place where folks is nice to me, that's all. Thomas an' the sheriff they're mean to me all the time. Real mean sometimes.'

'What about Grace?' John said.

'Gracie's nice. She sure is. But she can't stop Thomas an' the sheriff bein' mean to me. They take pleasure in it. I just can't be livin' like this no more.' Charity thought for a moment. 'If your wife is nice like you, she wouldn't mind havin' me around to help with the chores now, would she? I could do the sweepin', wash the floors, feed the chickens. Stuff like that. I could help with the cookin', if she'd let me.'

'I can't answer for her,' John said.

'Well,' Charity said. 'I best be gettin' back 'fore they notice I'm gone.'

She stood up and brushed the loose straw off her apron.

'You think on what I've offered you, mister. If you want me to tell you what I know, you come an' find me this evenin'. I'll be out the back of the saloon somewheres.' Looking straight ahead of her, she walked out of the stable into the evening light with a brisk, determined step.

9

'Whatdya mean, he jumped ya?' the sheriff screamed.

His neck was purple and the vein on the side of his head squirmed like a worm on a hook. He took a mighty kick at his desk and toppled it, sending Lincoln's Colts crashing down on to the floor. The desk drawers flew across the room, papers scattered and the sheriff's box of stogies burst open.

'Damnit to hell,' he yelled. 'Now look what you made me do!' He drew his gun and waved it at Lincoln. 'If a lawman can't rely on the army to help him, who can he rely on?'

He started to tip the desk upright.

'You wait till your colonel hears about this. He'll have you up on a charge. There's a bounty on Donnal's head.'

Lincoln sat on the bench, still locked in the cell.

'Why the hell did he send you on your own, anyways?'

'Colonel is out there tryin' to prevent the next Indian war, Sheriff,' Lincoln said calmly. 'I'll have to report that when I came to collect the prisoner, the sheriff o' Reckless wasn't nowhere to be found. An' where was he?' Lincoln answered his own question. 'In the saloon. Colonel's gonna be mighty impressed with that, ain't he?'

'Yeah, well,' the sheriff said. 'I can't be expected to sit in here all afternoon. Anyhow, the prisoner knew where I was.'

'The colonel's sure gonna like to hear that too,' Lincoln said. 'Now, are you gonna unlock this cell so's I can look for the prisoner, or are you gonna carry on hee-hawin' like a sick mule?'

The sheriff found the bunch of keys and let Lincoln out. Lincoln retrieved his guns from the floor and strode into the street, making sure he ground a couple of the sheriff's stogies under his boot heel as he went.

'What are you doin', Ma?' William had just come in from sweeping the barn. He wanted to get his chores out of the way early today. He planned to ask his mother if he could take the hunting rifle up to the woods.

Hannah was standing by the stove wearing a pair of John's pants, his spare shirt and an old saddle jacket she had found in the barn. Her hair was pushed up under her hat. There was a bedroll and a canteen on the table.

'I cooked up a real good stew, with chicken meat in it. I baked some bread. That should get you through a few days. After that, there's potatoes in the sack an' apples on the tree out back an' you'll have to rely on the traps. I got a bag of real good coffee. You can have that too.' Hannah spoke quickly, her words tumbling over each other. It made William nervous.

'Ma,' he asked again, 'what are you doin'?'

'There's some flour left, enough for two more loaves, an' you know where I keep the sourdough. But I don't suppose you'll feel like bakin' bread. You could make biscuits. That's easy enough.' Hannah was speaking more to herself than William. She put her arm around William and drew him to her. He let her hold him for a second, then pushed her away.

'Sit down, William,' she said. 'I gotta tell you somethin'.'

William sat at the table. 'You're scarin' me, Ma. Why're you actin like this?'

'You know old Mr Morgan at the store?' Hannah began.

'You know I do, Ma.'

'Well, he told me yesterday that there was a bank robbery in Calamity, on the day John was there.'

William's eyes widened. His questions tumbled out. 'Did Pa shoot the robbers? Is he OK?'

'William, I think John is in some kind of trouble.'

'You mean the robbers shot him, Ma? Is he all right?'

'No, it ain't that. I don't know what it is exactly. I think that Mikey Donnal has got some kinda hold over him.'

William's face clouded. 'It ain't to do with the accident, is it, Ma? With me shootin' Sean in the barn?'

'I don't think so, William. I ain't rightly sure what it is.' She paused and looked him. 'If he's in trouble, William, I gotta go to him. That means I gotta leave you here. You gotta look after the farm all by yourself. I want you to go and stay with the Morgans at the store. You're to sleep there each evenin'. You're to help Mr Morgan with whatever chores he wants you to and when you've finished up there, I want you to ride out here every day to feed the animals. Keep the place tidy an' make sure you shut the chickens in every night; we can't afford for a fox to take 'em.'

'But, Ma.'

'An' I want you to read your Bible, William. Every night. You read Jonah an' your favourite stories an' you imagine it's me readin' to you, like I usually do.'

'Ma, let me come with you. Please.'

'If somethin' happens,' Hannah continued, 'you tell Mr and Mrs Morgan. They're good people. They like us. John done Mr Morgan a good turn a year back when he saved the store from bein' robbed by that drifter. Mr Morgan would like to see you workin' down there with him, I reckon.'

'Please.'

'No, William. You gotta stay this time. You know I can't take you. If I go now, John is only a few days ahead. I'll head for Paradise Lake, on down to Reckless and south on the trail to Kansas after that. I'll catch up with him soon enough.'

'Why are you wearin' John's clothes, Ma?' William asked.

'If I can pass as a man from a distance, there's more chance I'll get left alone. I don't want to stand out.'

'You takin' a gun, Ma?'

Hannah hesitated. She heard the fear in William's question and spoke lightly. 'Well, we got a scatter-gun an' the huntin' rifle. Guess I'll take the scatter-gun and leave the big old hunting rifle for you. It's too heavy for me anyway.'

William was silent. He knew she didn't like him using the hunting rifle.

'I'll be back soon enough. A week or two, that's all.'

William's face was pale and set. All emotion was buried deep within him. He knew Hannah was doing what she had to. So must he.

'When will you be leavin', Ma?' William asked matter-of-factly, although he already knew the answer.

'I want you to go an' saddle up Runaway for me, right now.'

William went straight out to the barn without looking at her. Hannah picked up the bedroll and the canteen and took the shotgun down from its place on the chimney breast.

A few minutes later, William led Runaway out of the barn and handed her the reins. Hannah tried to put her arm around him again, but he pulled away. She mounted up and took a look back at the cabin. William turned and climbed up on to the porch.

'A week or two, William,' she called.

But he was already inside and did not answer.

Thomas laid his shotgun and two boxes of shells on the bar.

'Grace, you go an' find Charity and get her back in here,' he shouted. 'Then you get upstairs in the bedroom an' lock the door. You keep Charity away from the window, too. You hear a sound of anythin', you hide under the bed and stay there. Damn if I never heard o' nothin' like this. The army give the Sioux a reservation an' they jus' want their land back.'

Thomas started counting the shotgun shells. Grace ran out to look for Charity.

'She ain't out the back,' Thomas called after her. 'I already looked there.'

The street was full of soldiers and folks from the wagon train. The soldiers were helping the pioneers manhandle their wagons into the alleys between the buildings. The sturdiest ox-carts had been chosen to block both ends of the street. The whole town had been turned into a stockade. Colonel Pride and his adjutant rode their perfectly trained stallions up and down, noting how the defences were progressing and making the crowds part before them. People often cheered, or called out to the colonel as he passed. He acknowledged these greetings with a stern nod or a brief touch of the brim of his hat.

The atmosphere in the town was almost jubilant. From the time Colonel Pride first rode into town at the head of his column of troopers, the townsfolk and the pioneers were convinced that they had nothing to fear. Groups of men stood about outside the saloon. A few of them, holding shotguns over their arms, chatted to their friends as casually as if they were just about to go out shooting rabbits in a field. Some of the women had moved benches out of their wagons to sit together in the sunshine. Some laid the samplers they were working on across their laps and started sewing. Young children played at their feet and the older children ran shouting and laughing, weaving in and out of the crowd.

Lincoln took it on himself to patrol the perimeter. He crawled underneath a wagon jammed in one of the side alleys and walked the length of the street behind the buildings. He crossed over where the ox-carts blocked the end and walked back along the far side, making a full circle. He didn't like what he saw.

The Lakota Sioux were determined fighters. Lincoln admired them. The town's wooden buildings looked frail, perched out here on the magnificent open prairie. The young Sioux braves saw this vulnerable little place as an insult. Their chiefs had agreed, or been tricked into agreeing, to sign a paper so they had to leave the open plains and settle on a reservation. Then all these white men did was to disfigure the landscape with this collection of odd, ramshackle constructions.

Staring out over the plain, Lincoln watched for any sign of the Sioux. Of course, he didn't see anything. He didn't expect to. The town would be safe for a day, he thought. If the attack came, it would come at first light. But then, Lincoln reflected, the Sioux braves could just as easily decide that it was not worth risking the wrath of the tribal elders and simply head back to the reservation. Equally, they might decide just to throw a scare into the town, to ride round the perimeter a few times, at a safe distance, and then disappear into the landscape. It was impossible to tell. The main problem was that at the end of summer, every one of the houses was tinder dry. If the Sioux were in earnest, they would burn them out. With all the horses blockaded inside the town, the people would not be able to flee. The colonel's plan to turn the town into a stockade, could turn it into an inferno.

A pocket mouse skittered through the dry grass right by Lincoln's boots. It darted this way and that, stopping still to nibble at a grass stalk for a second before scurrying a few paces again. Lincoln looked down, amused by the tiny, nervous creature, concerned only with its little world of dust and stones and dry grass stalks. He stood still and let it scamper around his feet.

Something moved in the corner of his vision. The dappled brown head of a bull snake eased out from amongst the crisp grass. It paused and flicked out its tongue to taste the air. The mouse pranced among the stones. The bull snake leapt like a whip and caught it in its jaws. The snake gripped the tiny creature round its ribcage. Its tiny feet scrabbled; its black eyes stared. The bull snake coiled itself and with small deliberate movements eased the mouse into its throat. Within half a minute, the mouse was swallowed and the bull snake had slid back amongst the sun-bleached grass and disappeared.

'I bin lookin' for you.' Charity was breathless. 'Thomas wants me to stay inside the saloon. I told Gracie to say she couldn't find me. Thomas is gonna be mad again.'

John pulled Charity off the street, down an alley which had been blocked by a cart. 'With all this goin' on,' Charity continued, 'I didn't think you'd fin' me.'

'I gotta keep a watch out for the sheriff,' John said.

'You thought about what I said?'

'Yeah. I thought about it. I ain't so sure it's a good idea. I'm runnin' from the sheriff already. That means you will be too.'

'Well,' Charity said, 'I can't stand it here no more. If you ain't gonna take me, then I'll jus' give the money to some fella on the wagon train an' he'll take me.'

'All right,' John said. 'You just tell me where it is. I'll take you, since you're so determined to go anyways.'

'You promise you'll take me?' Charity said slyly.

'I said I would.'

'It's in the bank.'

'What?'

'Well, where else is a body gonna put a whole lot o' money?' Charity said. ' 'Course it's in the bank.'

'If it's stuck in some bank vault, I ain't gonna be able to get it then, am I?' John said. 'You think I'm takin' you with me for that?'

Charity laughed. 'It ain't in no vault. It's in the safe, stupid. That bank ain't got no vault.'

'You're just tryin' to trick me. I should seen that comin'. How d'you know the bank ain't got no vault anyways?'

'I bin in there. Thomas used to send me in there to see the old manager. He's dead now. Died of a heart attack. I ain't sorry neither. He was another one who was mean.'

'What are you tellin' me all this for?'

'That's the whole point,' Charity said. 'The manager was the only one who knew the combination for the safe. He wouldn't tell no one else. When he had his heart attack, they all looked round for the combination an' they couldn't find it.'

'How do you know all this?'

'How do you think I know? I was right there in his office when he had the heart attack.'

It took a minute for John to take this in.

'Now do you believe me?'

'An' the safe still ain't locked now?'

' 'Course it ain't. They just carry on using it and they don't tell nobody. I heard the deputy manager say that's what they'd do.'

Two troopers carrying Winchesters turned into the alley and took up a position on the ox-cart. They scanned the evening horizon for a sign of the Sioux.

'See anything?' John called.

'First light,' the trooper said. 'They always come at first light.'

10

At dawn, the town held its breath. The townsmen and the men from the wagon train were ready on the rooftops; the troopers took up firing positions on the wagons. The women from the wagon train defied the colonel's instructions and climbed up on to the roofs with the men. Some of them held Winchesters, and they took their children with them. All eyes stared over the plains, watching for a movement, anything which would tell them the braves were approaching. The children were silent and the dogs were quiet. As the first crack of blood-red light split the sky, everyone waited for the attack.

Suddenly, the chimes of a pocket watch rang out across the cool morning air from one of the rooftops. Soon afterwards, there was the sound of a window being smashed down in the street. Everyone heard these sounds, but no one moved from their firing positions or took their eyes off the prairie.

John had hidden under the straw in the stable and snatched a few hours' broken sleep. Satisfied that the town's attention was taken up with keeping watch for the Sioux, he slipped out of the stables and down the street to the bank.

He knocked a pane of glass out of a window with his elbow and reached inside to unfasten the sash. The breaking glass sounded like the sky falling on the silent street. He waited for someone to come running, but nobody did.

John raised the sash and climbed inside. He felt his way through a narrow doorway at the end of the counter and found the manager's office. The grey, steel safe with its array of dials and levers stood in front of him. He stood still and listened, trying to tell if anyone had figured where he was. A mouse scampered across the floor at his feet. He waited until the tiny scratching had died away.

As soon as John rested his hand on one of the levers of the safe door, it swung open silently. Inside were heaps of legal parchments tied with cotton tape, neatly folded deeds to the town's properties, a stack of black metal cash-boxes and piles of identical canvas money bags all bulging with dollars.

John took the bags of cash out of the safe one by one. The name of the bank was printed on the side of each bag in tall, black capitals. He examined each one until he came to a white bag, tied at the neck, stamped Property of Wells, Fargo Bank, Calamity, Minnesota' in blue ink. Underneath this bag was a small open tin. John picked it up and examined it. It contained five gold nuggets the size of the tips of his fingers. John replaced the tin and stacked the other bags back on top of it as silently as he could. He hugged the heavy cash bag close to his chest and pushed the safe door closed.

Outside, the darkness was beginning to lift. The street was still. Looking up, John could see the black silhouettes of the men on the rooftops against the purple sky. Keeping close to the side of the buildings, he hurried back to the livery stable as silently as he could and hid the bag deep in a pile of hay. Scarcely able to believe he had got away with it, he sat down on the straw to catch his breath.

Behind him in the shadows, John heard the unmistakable sound of a Colt being cocked. He froze. A voice spoke hoarsely to him through the darkness, from only a few feet away.

'You toss that pistol over by the door where I kin see it.'

John did as he was asked.

'That's right,' the voice breathed. 'Now you toss that money bag right out there too.'

John hesitated.

'Well, whatcha waitin' for? I kin put a hole in you easy as whistlin'.'

'You do that,' John said, 'you're gonna have the whole town down here.'

'You keep your voice down.'

The sheriff stepped forward into the half light.

'Anyone comes by, I just say I plugged an escaped bank robber who was tryin' to run out on us good people, just as we was bein' attacked by savages.' The sheriff laughed. 'You ain't putting nothin' over on me, Donnal. I aim to take that money an' collect the reward for you too.'

John pulled at the hay pile.

'Faster 'n that, damnit,' the sheriff snarled. 'Else I'm gonna have to shoot you and fin' the bag myself.'

'How d'you know I was here?' John said.

'Well,' the sheriff leered, 'let's just say the little songbird did some singin'.'

John raked amongst the straw until he uncovered the money.

'Now put these bracelets on.'

The sheriff threw a pair of handcuffs at John's feet. As John stooped to pick them up, he heard horses. Hoofbeats were thundering over the plain, still some way off, but approaching fast. Shots were fired from the rooftops. There was shouting. Women screamed. Then a sergeant's voice rang out, 'Hold your fire. Wait for the command.'

The stable horses stamped their feet in the stalls.

John picked up the handcuffs.

'Put them on,' the sheriff snarled.

They could hear war whoops of the braves above the sound of pounding hoofs. There was more shouting form the rooftops. Then the command came, 'Fire!'

The tight volley of rifle fire split the air.

'Wait for the command!' the sergeant called again. Then, a long minute later, 'Fire!'

A fusillade of shots from the rooftops followed.

Then there was a single blast from a shotgun. The sheriff was kicked forward with the force of both barrels. His gun flew out of his hand. He screamed in agony, face down in the hay. Grace stood in the doorway, a shotgun in her hands. She broke it open to reload and expertly slipped in two more cartridges.

'Now you turn over, Sheriff,' Grace said. 'I shot you in the back, now I'm gonna shoot you in the front, I swear.'

'Grace,' the sheriff implored, 'watcha doin?'

Another volley of disciplined rifle fire exploded. Then there was cheering from the rooftops.

The sheriff turned on to his side to look up at Grace. His face was drained. 'I ain't done nothin' to you. This is some kinda mistake, Grace.'

Graced looked at John. 'Charity just died,' she said. Her face was running with tears. 'I sat with her all night. The girl

102

could hardly talk, Sheriff beat her so bad last night. He made her tell about you an' how you was gonna take the money and take her away with you. Doctor said she was killed by bleedin' in the brain because he kept punchin' her in the head. Thomas was there. He saw 'im do it.'

'Grace, you gotta believe, I never intended—' the sheriff began.

Grace loosed off both barrels into the sheriff's chest. He fell back with red blood spattered around him over the yellow hay.

She turned to John. 'Charity said you're a good man. You do what you gotta.'

John collected his gun and the bag of money.

'You want me to help you hide the body?'

'No,' Grace said. 'Leave 'im for the rats. When they ask what I done, I'll say it was self-defence. After what he did to Charity last night, ain't no one gonna disbelieve me.' She paused. 'You leavin' town now?'

'Not right now,' John said. 'Something I gotta do first.'

John waited for Grace to leave the stable, then buried the bag of money under a pile of straw in the far corner.

Colonel Pride stood on the ox-cart blocking the end of Main Street smiling with satisfaction as he watched the Sioux ride away. He had summoned Lincoln to stand beside him so that he could give him the benefit of a full military assessment of the situation.

'We got 'em licked,' the colonel said. 'They ain't got the guts for a full-scale attack. They circled round a few times, makin' a lot of noise. That was the best they could do. They know they're no match for army Winchesters. Now they've rode off to the mountains.'

103

'Could be, Colonel,' Lincoln grunted.

The colonel sensed that Lincoln was unconvinced. 'You saw what happened, Scout. What other explanation could there be?'

'With the Sioux, there's always other explanations,' Lincoln said. 'We just saw what they wanted us to see, that's all.'

The retreating Sioux were far away now. The sound of their horses was gone; a cloud of white dust hung over where they had been on the plain.

'I could send a detachment after them,' the colonel reflected. 'But I don't want to provoke them. That would jeopardize the treaty.'

'Fighting Eagle knows that,' Lincoln said. 'He's got you all figured out, I reckon.'

'Damnit, man, say what you mean,' Colonel Pride snapped. 'The braves circled the town. They didn't dare to get in too close because of our superior fire power. When they saw the quality of our shooting, they turned tail and fled.'

'Then why have they headed north to the mountains and not east to the reservation?'

'Well, no one can tell that,' the colonel said.

'They had us boxed in here, Colonel. While we were concentrating on defending the town and the wagon train in here, we weren't watching what they were doin' out there. They didn't even try to hurt us. The Sioux are brave fighters, Colonel. They could have got in close if they'd wanted to.'

Colonel Pride jumped down off the cart and began to pace down Main Street, head bowed, hands clasped behind his back. Lincoln walked beside him. People from the wagon train called out congratulations. As far as they were

concerned, the colonel had seen off the Sioux and protected the train. Colonel Pride ignored them. He struggled
to make sense of what his scout was telling him.

'So you're telling me that getting us and the wagon train
into the town was a trick?'

'Could be a distraction,' Lincoln said.

'You're wrong,' Pride said. 'If we hadn't brought the
wagon train into the town, they would have been easy prey
out on the plains. They would all be dead by now.'

'Then why have the braves headed for the mountains,
Colonel? The Sioux are at home on the plains, they stay
away from the mountains. Maybe they wanted us all in the
town together. That's what I'm sayin'.'

'No. If Sioux braves get their blood up, they attack. We
were right to bring the wagons into town.'

'Let me follow them out to the mountains,' said Lincoln.
'It ain't no more than a two-day ride. I'll find out what
they're doin' up there and report back to you.'

A sergeant ran up to the colonel and saluted briefly. 'Sir,
I'm sorry to interrupt you. There's been a shooting. The
town sheriff has been shot. Happened this morning, sir,
while we was seein' off the damn Injuns.' The sergeant
grinned at the thought of their success.

'The sheriff? Whose side are these people on?' Colonel
Pride pulled himself together.

'Do they know who did it, Sergeant?'

'No, sir. But the saloon keeper says there was a prisoner
in the jail yesterday and he ain't there now. I checked.'

Pride snapped out his order. 'Find him and hang him,
Sergeant.'

'Yessir.' The sergeant saluted and turned smartly on his
heel.

Colonel Pride turned back to Lincoln.

'Two days,' he said. 'You can have two days to find out what the Sioux are doing in the mountains. I shall send a sergeant and a detachment of troopers with you. I shall also let the wagon train leave and provide a military escort as far east as Fort Trenton. That will take them past the reservation and well into the territories. You will easily be able to catch up with us, the ox-carts can barely make four miles a day. A third detachment will remain behind in the town.'

'You'll be splittin' your force, Colonel,' Lincoln said.

'Thank you, Scout,' Pride said. 'When I wish you to pass comment on my strategy I shall ask you. Carry on.'

Colonel Pride turned away from Lincoln and beckoned to his lieutenant who had been waiting for his orders at a respectful distance.

Hannah emerged from the woodland on to the shore of Lake Paradise. It was evening. Golden light reflected off the water. A family of loons drifted across the surface. Oaks and maples cascaded down the mountainside to the lake. The blaze of red and yellow leaves promised a hard winter. Hannah dismounted and led Runaway to drink from the lake. She knelt at the waterside and filled her canteen.

Since leaving the farm, Hannah had not seen a soul. She had by-passed Calamity and headed straight on to the grassland heading south, spending most of the journey trying not to think about William. Each time thoughts about him stole into her mind, she pushed them aside. He would be fine, she told herself. He knew how to work the traps, and apart from keeping the place tidy, there was little enough to do on the farm. Anyway, Mr Morgan would keep an eye on him.

Hannah sat down on the shore and watched the water birds bobbing like black and white corks on the surface of the lake. She drank from her canteen and thought about John. He was a good man. He cared for her and for William and did his best to provide for them. He loved her. But up against Mikey, he seemed young, a boy almost, as if his goodness made him vulnerable.

Hannah understood why Lincoln had left the farm for the frontier life, but she did not forgive him for it. He had wanted her to go with him and she had considered it. But it would have meant living in a fort and bringing up William with the troopers and the constant threat of Indian wars all around them. It would have meant being the scout's half-breed wife. They had built the cabin. She could survive there. William was with her, so she had let Lincoln go.

The Civil War came and went. It hardly touched Wilderness County. She learned news of battles in places she had not heard of from gossip in the store. Some of the local men went off to fight. Some of them did not return. She concentrated on raising William, on doing her best with the farm, on keeping the cabin roof repaired. Then the war was over. People in Calamity were happy because the Union had won, but they still looked at her in the same way because of her Sioux blood. She would always be an outsider.

The following year, John came looking for work, a hollow-eyed young man, haunted by memories of fighting and prison. He had half an idea that he could claim some land and start a farm somewhere, as far away from his past as he could get. He worked for his keep for a whole summer and slept in the barn. He knew nothing about farming, but he worked the traps. William liked him. He was company and he was kind.

Something startled the loons and they blundered into the air, thrashing their clumsy wings against the surface of the water. Hannah turned. Six Sioux braves were standing behind her at the edge of the wood. Three of them were covering her with Winchesters. They wore buckskin shirts decorated with red and blue war beads. They peered at her curiously for a moment. Then one of them laughed aloud, ran forward and knocked her hat off. Her black hair tumbled down over her shoulders. He turned to the others and said something. Realizing she was a woman, they shouted with surprise and lowered their weapons.

One of the braves beckoned her to follow them back into the woods. She shook her head and pointed to the ground to show that she was staying where she was. He looked shocked for a moment then walked across to her, swung his arm back and slapped her across the face, seized a bunch of her hair and dragged her towards the edge of the wood. Blood welled from her nose. The brave shouted a brief command to one of the others who grabbed her horse by the bridle and towed it after them.

11

When a sergeant led a detachment of men into the livery stable to collect the sheriff's body, they gave the building a cursory search. John guessed they had orders to look for him, but the only people in the town who could identify him were Thomas, the saloon keeper, and Grace.

As the troopers had entered, John slipped out through a rear door. He walked up the side of the stables to the street, lay on his back underneath a wagon and pretended to examine an axle. The sergeant and some of the soldiers peered at him as they passed and then moved on. John was right. They didn't know what he looked like. Even so, he decided to lie low in the barn for the rest of the day.

Now, John lay in the mezzanine loft listening to two men argue. They were directly below him, their faces hidden by the broad brims of their hats. Both spoke with a heavy Alabama drawl.

'You just gotta be patient, Brother,' one of them said, 'If we set out now, we're gonna be advertisin' ourselves. We're gonna attract the attention of the whole wagon train and the army too.'

'I'm not sayin' we should just leave. We'll go to the

colonel an' explain that the wagon is carryin' perishable items an' that we gotta. Like I always said, we shouldn't have joined the damn wagon train in the first place.'

'Colonel Pride won't agree to that. He won't let no one go without an escort and he ain't gonna provide an escort unless it's for the whole train. Anyhow,' the first man added, 'we start talkin' about our wagon, it's gonna draw folks' attention to it. Then they're gonna start wonderin' why it's so heavy an' slow when it's just carryin' a load o' plants.'

'I'm tellin' you,' the first man insisted, 'we're already two days behind. One more day an' we're gonna miss that rendezvous with Fighting Eagle. We miss that an' he's gonna be sore as hell. I know people who've done business with 'im before. He's gonna say we broke the agreement and he's gonna want a whole reduction on the price of them rifles. We could end up with diddly.'

'Well, there ain't nothin' we kin do fer now. I reckon we should get ourselves up to the saloon an' have a drink. Ain't no one gonna touch the wagon.'

The man pulled a watch out of his waistcoat pocket and opened the lid.

Immediately, a sweet chiming melody filled the stable.

'Three o'clock,' the man sighed. 'Time passes slower'n a dead rattlesnake when you're waitin' for somethin' to happen.'

He rested his arm on his brother's shoulder as they stepped out of the shadows of the stable and into the sunlight. John waited for a few minutes then climbed down the ladder from the hay loft and followed the two men out into the street. He saw them pause by one of the newer-looking wagons and then stroll on towards the saloon. John followed, looking down at the ground, making sure he didn't catch anyone's eye.

John hauled himself up on to the tail board of the wagon and peered inside. The whole wagon was filled with young fruit trees, their roots wrapped in sacking. John recognized apricots, peaches, lemons and oranges. John had heard of pioneers doing this, taking a wagonload of saplings out West to start a farm. It was good cover. John also noticed that the floor to the wagon was unusually high. He had to take a look. He crawled in amongst the saplings, pushed them aside and started to lever up a floorboard with his hunting knife. He was surprised by the ease with which he was able to free it. Underneath the floor was a compartment crammed with long wooden cases. The Preacher was planning to sell Winchesters to the Sioux.

The war party had not bothered to hide their tracks. They headed due north from Reckless to the mountains. Lincoln and the troopers followed, riding hard over the prairie. Lincoln knew two days was too short a time to catch up with them and report back. The colonel had listened to his advice and ignored it. He had split his force.

Pride always underestimated the Sioux. Lincoln was beginning to suspect that Fighting Eagle, the Sioux chief, had planned this all along. Fighting Eagle might be trying to make Pride believe that there were more Sioux in the mountains. Maybe the braves hadn't covered their tracks because they wanted to be followed. The Sioux chief knew the colonel had complete faith in his Winchesters. He knew the military always believed rifles would always provide victory over courage and cunning. He also knew that the colonel could be wrong.

By late afternoon, Lincoln was leading the troopers up

the lower slopes of Pearl Mountain. He knew the paths. The Sioux war party were headed over the ridge to Lake Paradise. Still on the southern side of the ridge, he tethered his horse and told the troopers to wait for him while he went on ahead. He debated whether to take his Winchester and decided to leave it in its saddle holster, leaving both his hands free. He still had his Colts if there was any trouble. Lincoln left the main track and trod lightly through the undergrowth.

The Sioux were camped behind the tree-line, close to the lake shore. Lincoln could hear them before he could see them. Their voices carried clearly through the trees. It sounded like they had met up with another raiding party. Lincoln had to get closer to make an assessment of their numbers. He had not expected to come across them so soon.

Lincoln circled round behind where the Sioux were, keeping to higher ground and searching for a break in the trees to give him a view of their camp. The smell of wood smoke and fish being cooked over a fire hung in the air. Judging by their shouts and laughter, the braves had not realized he was so close and hadn't given a thought to setting a guard.

Pulling himself up on to the lower branches of a maple, Lincoln was able to see the braves. They were sitting round a low fire waiting for their fish to cook. Rows of yellow walleyes were skewered on willow wands and suspended over the fire. Lincoln counted eight braves, though there seemed to be others there out of his view. Their ponies stood a little way off.

One brave, wearing a Stetson and saddle jacket sat with his back to Lincoln. His long black hair spilled down over his shoulders. The others seemed to be teasing him. Lincoln couldn't hear the answers he was giving, but it seemed to be the cause of great hilarity. Eventually the fish was ready. One of the braves indicated that the Sioux in the western clothes should hand them round. As he stood up, Lincoln saw that he was wearing buckskin pants and was barefoot. The brave handed a skewered fish to each of the others in turn. As he turned back to the fire, Lincoln saw that it wasn't a Sioux brave, it was Hannah. She took the last walleye for herself and sat down to eat with the others.

'Hey!'

There was a shout behind him and someone seized John's leg and jerked him backwards out of the wagon raking an armful of fruit trees with him. He fell face down on to the street in a pile of saplings. He took the force of the fall on his rib cage. It kicked the breath out of him. Someone hauled him upright and sat him against the wagon wheel.

'I bin watchin' you,' the man yelled. He was huge. Chest like a barrel, hands like hams. He wore a dirty shirt and a broad leather belt around his waist. He leaned his great boot against John's chest, keeping him pinned against the wheel. John recognized him as the owner of the wagon parked up behind the Preacher's. His wife, a pinch-faced woman with her hair drawn back severely, appeared beside him covering John with a shotgun.

'I seed you earlier, crawlin' underneath the wagons, pretendin' to inspect the axles. We bin advised to look out fer thieves when we pulled into this here town.'

The man's boot was practically cracking John's ribs.

'Lemme speak, mister,' John gasped.

The man took his boot off John's chest. Air flooded back into his lungs. The man leaned down and hauled John to his feet. Instead of listening to what he had to say, he swung his great fist back and smashed John in the jaw. It was like being hit with an anvil. The world spun inside John's head. A second blow slammed into his guts and tore the air out of him. He slumped down on to the ground, against the wagon wheel, and lay gagging in an attempt to breathe again.

The woman said, 'Want me to let 'im have both barrels, Merve? Make an example?'

'Nope. Best way to do that is to let the troopers have 'im. You let me have the scatter-gun an' run up there and fin' the sergeant.'

'Mister—' John began again.

Merve leaned down and jabbed the stock of the shotgun into John's face, breaking his nose. Pain lanced through his head. He covered his face with his hands. Blood washed down over his mouth.

'You ain't makin' no weasel excuses. I caught you red-handed. You kin just shut up an' wait fer the troopers to haul you off to jail.'

John's head swam. Excited voices surrounded him and he heard running footsteps. One of his eyes was swelling shut. Someone pulled John's hand away from his face.

'Lemme take a look at 'im.'

John recognized the Preacher's voice. The same leering face John remembered from Andersonville was looking down at him.

'Well, he sure ain't pretty. You done a good job there, Merve. Lucky fer him it was you caught 'im an' not me. I woulda blowed 'is head right off.'

114

The Preacher climbed up on to the tailboard of the wagon.

'Somebody pass these trees up to me, will ya? Sonofabitch sure has made a mess in here.'

A crowd of people from the wagon train had gathered. Some of them passed the saplings up to the Preacher, who made a great show of arranging them carefully in his wagon; some of them spat at John as he lay crumpled and in pain by the wagon wheel; some of them merely gawped at him. They all looked hurt and horrified that someone should steal from one of the wagons. Full of self-righteous anger, some of them muttered about lynching. Big Merve stood over John, shotgun in hand, like a hunter over a trophy kill.

The sergeant and a trooper came running up. They drew their Navy Colts and ordered John to his feet. John obeyed, still shielding his face with his hands. The sergeant jabbed him in the kidneys with his pistol and shoved him down the street towards the jail.

The branch gave way with an ear-splitting crack. Lincoln crashed to the ground dragging the broken branch and swathes of undergrowth with him. He was dazed for a moment and then started to pick himself up. He heard the Sioux braves shout and then heard them dash through the woods towards him. They surrounded him almost before he had got to his feet.

Two of them aimed Winchesters at his chest. Others were shouting at him, shocked by his sudden appearance, but their words spilled out too fast for him to understand. Still others fanned out into the woods to see if Lincoln had anyone with him. The braves with the rifles shoved him down the slope in the direction of the camp.

Lincoln saw the shock of recognition in Hannah's eyes, but she looked away from him and said nothing. She began clearing up the remains of the fish where the braves had dropped it on the ground when they heard Lincoln's branch break. She did not look at Lincoln or make eye contact with any of the braves. She just carried on clearing up the campsite like any squaw would do. Lincoln noticed that she was tethered to a tree with strips of plaited hide tied round one ankle. The leash was just long enough for her to cook and tend the fire.

The braves were arguing amongst themselves about what to do with Lincoln. One of them kept poking him in the chest with the barrel of his Winchester, his eyes blazing. Others were clearly trying to dissuade the brave from shooting him. One of them kept pushing the rifle barrel aside. Eventually, the brave spat at Lincoln's feet, put the rifle down and walked away.

Another brave kicked Lincoln's legs away from under him and he tumbled backwards. Hannah sat on the far side of the fire not looking at any of them, trying to be invisible. One of the braves took Lincoln's Peacemakers from his holsters, tossed them into the undergrowth and kept him covered with a Winchester.

When the braves who had gone off to search the woods returned, the war party relaxed. Still keeping Lincoln covered, they kept glancing at him and argued among themselves. He had surprised them, so they were not sure how to react. This made him certain that Fighting Eagle wanted the army to know that there were Sioux on the mountain. His theory was correct: this was a trick to entice Colonel Pride to split his force three ways. This group of braves was the bait. They were going to keep him alive to take the message back to Pride.

The braves sat down by the embers of the fire and the tone of their discussion became calmer. Then one of them stood up suddenly and walked over to Hannah, screamed at her and pointed at the dying fire. She appeared confused for a moment and the brave raised his foot and stamped at her with his heel and screamed again. She pushed herself back out of range of the kicks and scrambled to her feet. She immediately began to forage for dead sticks in the undergrowth, stretching at the length of the line of hide. The brave spat at her and took his seat with the others.

As Lincoln watched, the braves took out their whetstones and began to sharpen their blades. They spoke quietly to each other as they worked and compared the sharpness of the knives when they had finished. Every now and again, one of them would glance at Lincoln, as if they were still talking about him. The cry of a screech owl tore the air like a scream of pain and made the braves look up for a moment, then they returned to their work.

After a while, one of the braves held his knife up to the firelight. He examined the sharpness of the blade from different angles then held it by the tip of the blade in his right hand. He weighed it for a moment and then, without appearing to take aim, threw it across the fire into the trunk of the maple a foot above Lincoln's head. The blade struck the centre of the trunk and lodged deep in the young wood. Lincoln gasped with surprise. The other braves murmured admiringly and grinned to each other.

The brave barely looked at Lincoln as he strolled over to retrieve his blade. He said something sharply to the Sioux covering Lincoln with the Winchester, hauled Lincoln to

117

his feet and shoved him back against the trunk of the tree. One brave pressed the barrel of the Winchester against his chest while the other pulled his arms behind the trunk of the maple and tied them. Lincoln instinctively pulled away. The Winchester jabbed him hard in the chest. Other braves got to their feet and held Lincoln while his feet were bound to the trunk of the tree. Finally, a strip of hide was tightened around Lincoln's forehead and tied behind the tree trunk forcing him to look at the group of Sioux round the fire. The braves spoke quietly to each other and went back to preparing their blades by the fire.

Lincoln saw Hannah look up and, in the flickering fire-light, saw terror written across her face.

12

'You're John Wright, ain't you?'

The trooper who had escorted John to the jailhouse the previous afternoon pushed a tin cup of water through the bars. He stood back and let John get up from the wooden bench and take the water. Early morning light filtered though the cell window.

'Who wants to know?'

'I knowed it was you,' the trooper said. 'John Wright, First Battalion New York Sharpshooters. I knowed it. You don' recognize me?'

John peered at the trooper through his swollen eye.

'Can't say I do.' John slumped back down on the bench and leaned against the wall. His body smouldered with pain: his head still rang from the crack with the shotgun; his ribs were bruised from being hauled out of the wagon; his guts were sore from Merve's fist.

'Sure you do,' the trooper persisted. 'We was in Andersonville together. Harrison Bean, Second Infantry.' The trooper grinned at him. 'That day you was runnin' from the guards Mikey Donnal an' his brother hid you. I was right there. Right beside 'em. Them guards walked on

119

by an' didn't notice you at all.'

John looked hard at the trooper, trying to recall his face.

'I stayed on in the army after the war,' Bean said. 'That's how come I'm here now. Every now an' again I run into someone from Andersonville. People turn up outa nowhere, like you jus' done.'

'You know this Mikey Donnal?' John said.

'Ain't seen 'im since Andersonville. He was a friendly fella.'

'I heard there was a price on 'is head,' John said.

'Happened to a lot o' guys,' Bean agreed. 'War ended and they couldn't settle to nothin'. Went on the trail an' took to the bad. Like you, thievin' from wagons.' Bean brightened. 'Not me. I stayed on as a regular trooper. Proud of it.'

John ignored the slur.

'You remember a guard in Andersonville called the Preacher?' John said.

'Sure wouldn't forget 'im. He was one of the meanest sonsabitches I ever come across.'

'Well, I been on his trail. There's a price on his head, too. I trailed him right here to Reckless.'

'Yeah?' Bean said. 'He here now? I ain't seed 'im.'

'Well, he's here all right.'

'Price on 'is head, is there? I ain't surprised at that. Where is he?'

'You're gonna have to help me get outa here 'fore I tell you that.'

Bean paused. 'I could get word to the colonel. Have to be quick though because the wagon train's gettin' ready to leave. He's gonna send an escort with them to Fort Trenton. That's the kinda guy he is. He was pretty riled this mornin'' though because one of the wagons left during the night without his permission. He wasn't pleased by that at all.'

'You goin' with the wagons?' John said.

'I'm in the detachment that's stayin' in town.'

'Tell the colonel I got some information about men sellin' guns to the Sioux.'

'He's sure gonna want to hear that. I know it. Anybody brought you any food?'

'Nope,' John said. 'Sure could do with a bite to eat.'

'That's what I reckoned. I'll see what I kin rustle up.' Bean headed for the door.

'Just tell the colonel,' John called after him. 'I ain't talkin' to no one but him. Tell 'im I mean to claim the reward.'

With a square of blue sky showing through the barred window, John sat down on the wooden bench to wait.

Half an hour later Colonel Pride stood on the porch of the saloon looking down at John's bruised face, trying to decide whether or not he was telling the truth. It was eleven in the morning. The troopers were mounted up. The wagon train was ready to roll.

Just as the colonel had been about to give the order for the wagons to move out, a sergeant had brought him a message about gunrunners. This was something Pride could not afford to ignore. He ordered the man to be brought to him.

Colonel Pride suspected it was just another attempt by a thief, who had been caught red-handed, to get himself released from jail. He listened to the man's unlikely story, trying to decide whether to take it seriously. To search the whole wagon train would take hours. Pride was minded to ignore the story, head on out and have the man thrown back in jail to await summary justice on his return.

But one thing made the colonel hesitate. The man claimed to have been in Andersonville during the war. He also claimed that the man he alleged was running guns had been an Andersonville guard. This struck a chord with the colonel. His own beloved brother had died in Fort Sumpter, Andersonville, Georgia, a month before the war ended. Even though, as a military man, the colonel was used to death, he had never been able to forget the stories of the brutality that went on there. Imaginings of how his brother must have suffered haunted his dreams.

The colonel signalled to his lieutenant to have the men dismount. The order was passed down the column. The troopers stood easy beside their horses. Pride gestured John and the lieutenant to walk with him. If the man could identify the wagon, as he claimed, there would be no need to search the whole column.

The three men walked the length of the wagon train. The pioneers stared down at John with contempt. By the time they reached the last wagon, just as Colonel Pride had suspected, the prisoner had failed to pick out a wagon.

'I heard a wagon left during the night,' John said. 'That must be the one.'

Colonel Pride stared at him.

'Colonel, I'm tellin' you, there's a cargo of fruit trees an' underneath it there's enough cases o' Winchesters to arm a war party.'

'Fruit trees,' the colonel repeated. He turned to the lieutenant. 'Find a wagon with a cargo of fruit trees and search it.' His voice was curt. He was running out of patience.

'You won't find it,' John insisted. 'It'll be the one that

122

headed out.'

'Then find someone who knows about these fruit trees,' the colonel called after the lieutenant. 'And bring him here on the double.'

The colonel turned to John and lowered his voice. 'When you were in Andersonville, did you ever come across a young lieutenant with the 13th Pennsylvania Volunteers, name of Henry Pride?'

'No, sir, can't say I did.' John looked at the colonel. 'I'm sorry, sir.'

'No matter,' the colonel said, and looked away.

A man pushed his way through the line of wagons, calling out to the colonel.

'Colonel Pride, sir. That's the man, sir. That's the man who broke out of jail and shot the sheriff.' It was Thomas from the saloon. 'He robbed a bank up in Calamity, north o' Pearl Mountain. Sheriff arrested 'im for it. He busted out somehow. Musta went after the sheriff.'

Colonel Pride held up his hand to silence the man. He looked with contempt at this wild-eyed civilian with whiskey on his breath.

'Sheriff did arrest me, Colonel,' John said. 'But I never robbed no bank. Sheriff arrested me because he thought there was a price on my head, which there ain't.'

The colonel's voice rang out. 'We have no more time to waste. Lieutenant, prepare to lead a detachment after the wagon which set out during the night and search it.' He indicated John. 'Take this man with you.'

'Sir, I mean to go after him myself,' John protested. 'It's what I came here to do.'

'I'll allow no more bounty-hunting. You can put all thoughts of a reward out of your head. My troopers will deal with the man. This is an army matter now.'

Colonel Pride turned to Thomas, full of condescension. 'You, get back to your saloon-keeping. I have no information that this man is a bank robber. He fought an honourable war. He will now be assisting the military. If you have evidence to the contrary, I shall consider it. In the meantime, be minding your tongue with unfounded scuttlebutt, sir.'

'We was all in the war, Colonel,' Thomas protested.

Pride fixed him with an unflinching stare. 'And which regiment were you in, Saloon-keeper?'

Thomas's eyes rolled wildly. He clicked his heels and came to attention as if he was on parade. 'First Missouri Infantry, sir.'

Colonel Pride stiffened. 'I thought so,' he said. 'You best get back to your saloon.'

'He killed the sheriff,' Thomas moaned. 'You can't let 'im get away.'

Grace stepped forward from between the wagons. 'He didn't kill the sheriff, Colonel Pride, I did.'

Pride exploded, 'What kind of people are you? You come to me with your accusations and no proof. I got an ex-Johnny Reb infantryman callin' this man a liar with not a shred of evidence to back it up. Now I got a woman sayin' she's committed a murder. An' do you have the proof for this, madam?'

'No I don't, Colonel,' Grace said. 'But I can tell you why I done it.'

'And why would that be? And why would you confess to it anyways?'

'The sheriff beat my friend so bad, she died,' Grace said. 'I kin prove it too. Thomas saw it all, didn't you, Thomas?'

'Why, yes, I did.' Thomas was cowed in the face of the authority of Grace's words. He stared at the ground. 'Charity died,' he said.

'When the sheriff started on me in the livery stables this mornin',' Grace continued, 'I shot 'im. Wasn't no more than he deserved an' I ain't sorry for it.' Grace looked Colonel Pride directly in the eye. 'I ain't got no proof of it, Colonel. Only my word.'

'I ain't got time for this. None of us has,' Pride thundered. 'There's a wagon train ready to roll; there's a wagon out there likely selling firearms to the Indians; the scout ain't returned from Pearl Mountain and Fighting Eagle means to attack. I have military matters to deal with. I am a military man.' He waved Grace away and strode, red-faced, up the street. His lieutenant kept well back and John followed. When Pride reached the head of the column, he had composed himself.

He turned to the lieutenant. 'Start out right away and find this wagon. Take four men and this civilian with you. He will be able to make the identification. If there are rifles on board, arrest the men and escort the wagon back to town.'

He turned to John. 'I shall require you to ride out with the troopers to identify this gunrunner. I want to know if it is the Andersonville guard.' The colonel looked hard at John. 'I must emphasize that there will be no bounty now. You have to bring a wanted man in without the help of the army to claim a reward.'

He beckoned to the sergeant. 'Detail two troopers to head north to look for the scout. If they don't find him within two days, tell them to turn south and catch up with the wagons. Tell them to stay on the lookout for any signs of a war party. Lieutenant Carson and Sergeant Fife will take a detachment and escort the wagon train to Fort Trenton. A detail will stay here commanded by me, as protection for the town. Carry on.'

The colonel looked at John. Then he beckoned Trooper Bean over.

'Escort this man to the livery stable to collect his horse. Then bring him back to the column.'

In the stable, Bean helped John saddle his horse. John thanked him and, at the same time, launched a mighty right-hand punch which caught Bean on the tip of his jaw, lifted him off his feet and sent him flying back into the straw. He was out cold.

'Didn't want to do that,' John said, 'but there ain't no other way.'

John sneaked back up the street to the sheriff's office to collect his gunbelt. When he returned to the stable, Trooper Bean lay peacefully in the straw. John mounted up and galloped out of town. He had to claim the bounty for Hannah, for William and for the unborn child. And he had come to avenge Billy, his childhood friend. He had to take the Preacher down, alone.

13

Hannah barely slept. Terror stalked her dreams. The breeze in the branches above her, a spit of damp wood in the fire, a brave stirring in his sleep: all these things threw her into consciousness, awake and aware of any movement in the camp. The hide rope left a raw, bloody circle round her ankle. The pain of it never left her. Every time she opened her eyes, she focused on Lincoln. The strip of hide had slipped off his forehead. He was slumped forward like a corpse.

The braves woke before dawn and took their fishing spears down to the edge of the lake. They barely glanced at the scout. The last brave to leave the camp, kicked Hannah and nodded towards the fire which was now a pile of ash. The air was sharp and dampness from the lake was in the woods. The grey beginnings of day filtered through the trees.

Hannah struggled to her feet, her limbs tight with cold, the bruises from the braves' kicks burning along her arm. She began to forage for firewood at the edge of the camp. She could hear the braves moving about by the lake, keeping their voices low. No one was watching her.

Lincoln's Peacemakers were still in the brush where the brave had discarded them the previous evening. They were out of her reach unless she could cut the strips of hide round her ankle. Lincoln was still slumped forward. She threw a tiny pebble at his feet. He jerked upright at once, his eyes fixed on her.

Lincoln nodded to a tree on the far side of the fire. One of the braves had left his bow and quiver of arrows propped against it. Hannah found a stick long enough to reach and hooked the quiver towards her, over the fire. She took out an arrow and tossed the quiver back, aiming for its place against the tree. The quiver struck the tree trunk and upended, spilling arrows out over the ground. Hannah's heart exploded in her chest. She looked wildly at Lincoln. He shook his head. 'Don't think about it', his look said. 'Stay calm'.

Hannah sawed at the plaited hide round her ankle with the arrow head. The leather was supple and strong. The point of the flint arrow head was sharp, but it was not a cutting tool. She sat on the ground and worked with tiny, desperate strokes. There was a noise in the undergrowth. Hannah snatched some wood and threw it on the fire, stood up and began to gather twigs from round the site again. She shoved the arrow inside the leg of her pants.

A brave stepped into the clearing. He said something, but Hannah did not look up. She was shaking with fear. The brave nudged her shoulder to get her attention. She looked up at him. He was grinning proudly and holding out three walleye impaled on his spear to show her. He slid the fish off the spear on to the ground where they writhed helplessly in the dust.

Still grinning, the brave pointed at the fire. Hannah

nodded. Then she pulled at the leash around her ankle to show she could not walk far enough to gather wood. The brave shrugged, pulled a knife from his belt, stooped down and cut the leash. He pointed to the fire again. Then he took his spear and started back down through the undergrowth towards the lake.

Hannah ran round the fire to Lincoln. She sawed at the leather strips binding his wrists behind the tree.

'Hurry,' he breathed. 'They ain't gonna be long.'

She sawed desperately at the leather strips. Time slowed down. It was taking her an age to make any progress. She tried a small slashing motion against the leather; she kept turning the arrowhead to use both sides; nothing seemed to work. Then, suddenly, the hide gave way: Lincoln's hands were free.

There were voices again and a crashing in the undergrowth. Hannah pressed the arrow into Lincoln's hand behind the tree and turned to collect up the spilled arrows. She had just time to replace the quiver against the tree trunk when two more braves returned. Both of them were laughing and carrying fish on their spears. When they saw the fire was not made and the other fish were still on the ground, their mood changed to irritation. They shouted at her and pointed to the pile of ash. One of them took a few half-hearted kicks at her while she knelt to pile kindling on the embers and blow on it to make a flame. They looked at Lincoln, slumped forward with his arms behind the tree. As the food was not ready, they left their fish for her and strolled back down to the lake.

Lincoln slid down the tree trunk and sat on the ground, sawing at the leather ties around his ankles with the arrowhead. Hannah built up the fire and arranged the fish over it. She piled firewood and found a branch to sweep around the fire to make some kind of neatness in the camp, hoping it would distract the braves.

John rode hard through the waist-high prairie grass. He kept glancing back over his shoulder, expecting to see a column of troopers pursuing him. There was no one. Maybe the army hadn't realized he had given them the slip; maybe Colonel Pride had decided it was not worth chasing one man. The land looked as flat as an ocean, but John knew that the rise and fall were deep enough to hide a column of horsemen. It was always possible that they were coming for him.

Up ahead there was nothing but miles of tall grass moving in the breeze. Waves of shimmering green and silver were broken by patches of grey prairie smoke and pale onion flowers. A falcon wheeled high in the morning air searching for its prey. John slowed to rest his horse. He scanned the horizon for a sign of the wagon. Eventually, from the top of a rise, he saw it. The canvas cover lurched from side to side as the wooden wheels rode the rough ground.

Watching the wagon making its awkward progress over the land, John thought of Hannah and the farm. The bounty would bring them prosperity: a new plough, another horse, seed for the coming year, even a little money in the bank. They would be able to build a future. He remembered Andersonville: waking with a blade at his throat, the crushing weight of the guard pinning him down; Billy, struggling with the Preacher, and the terrible, heart-breaking sigh he gave as the Confederate bayonet slid into his chest. Then he recalled the Preacher leering down from the pigeon coop with Billy's watch chiming in his hand.

There was still no sign of the troopers. The empty prairie spread for miles in all directions. The midday sun was overhead. Some way off, the falcon hovered over its prey. John watched the wagon jolting from side to side. There was nowhere for the Preacher to hide.

John cupped his hands around his mouth. 'Preacher,' he yelled. The breeze took his shout and flung it away. The wagon rumbled on.

John urged his horse on until he drew alongside the driver's seat. The Preacher had the reins in his hands and a Winchester across his knees. His brother sat beside him. The Preacher shoved the reins into his brother's hands and pointed the rifle at John.

'I got business with you,' John said.

'Business?' The Preacher looked confused. He scanned the grassland to see if John was on his own. John saved him the trouble.

'There ain't nobody here but me. You got somethin' o' mine and I'm askin' you for it.'

'You're talkin' crazy. I don't know you.'

'I ain't got much time,' John said. 'The army's after me. If they follow me here they're gonna find you too.'

The Preacher hesitated.

'You got a watch that rightfully belongs to me. You took it off my friend the night you killed him in Andersonville.'

'You followed me all the way out here because of a watch?' The Preacher was amazed. 'Wait a minute,' he said. 'I do know you. You're the fella that broke into the wagon back in Reckless.'

'And I come to claim the bounty on your head.'

As he spoke, John wheeled his horse behind the wagon.

131

The shot from the Preacher's Winchester went wide. John galloped back up the ridge and jumped out of the saddle into the prairie grass. Shots screamed past his head. John pulled his Colt from its holster and kept below the height of the grass. The Preacher continued firing blind. With his wagon overloaded, there was no question of them trying to outrun a horseman. He had to stand and fight.

Hauling himself along on his elbows, John circled around to the far side of the wagon. He raised his head and peered over the top of the grass. The Preacher and his brother were lying underneath the wagon, Winchesters ready. John took a shot and ducked back below the level of the grass. A storm of rifle fire blasted back. John kept low and crawled on. He raised his head again and fired. Another volley answered from under the wagon.

This kept this up for some time. John fired, ducked down into the grass and a hail of bullets replied. Then John noticed that only one rifle was returning fire. He was sure he hadn't hit either the Preacher or his brother. One of them must be circling around behind him.

John kept low, edged to the other side of the wagon and made his way up to the rise. This gave him a clear view, but he was too far away for an accurate shot. He was right though. He could see the long grass moving as someone crawled through it heading for the spot he had last fired from. John could also see the barrel of a Winchester poking out between the spokes of one of the rear wagon wheels. He had to choose. He could either get within range of the guy in the grass, or he could try to take out the man underneath the wagon. No choice: the wagon was closer.

Just as he was about to set off crawling through the grass, he heard the sound of a Winchester being cocked next to his head. He felt the cold hard jolt of the barrel being pressed up against the back of his head. John flipped himself sideways and kicked out backwards. The shot from the Winchester went into the ground next to his shoulder. A man yelled and tumbled down on top of him, before he could fire again. It was the Preacher's brother.

Still lying on top of him, the man grabbed John by the throat and jerked his head backwards as if he was trying to tear it off. John jabbed him in the guts with his elbows. His huge belly protected him. Then John knocked one of his arms aside and punched him in his fleshy neck. But the angle was wrong and he couldn't get enough force behind the blow. His fist slipped off the greasy skin. The man leaned down on him. John was enveloped in his putrid breath. Before John realized what the man was doing, he had bitten off the top of John's left ear.

John howled as pain clawed through him. The man leaned back, roared with crazy pleasure and spat the gristle into the grass. John gathered all his strength, heaved him aside, grabbed the Colt out of his holster and fired three times. The Preacher's brother crashed down beside him like a felled ox, blood dripping from his mouth.

'Silas,' the Preacher yelled.

John staggered to his feet. The Preacher was running towards him, a Winchester in his hand. He fired from the hip and the shot went wide.

'Where's Silas? What you done to him?'

John ignored the burning pain and the blood running down the side of his face, took careful aim with his Colt and fired. The Preacher's Winchester jerked out of his hand and spun away into the grass. The Preacher stopped dead.

'Ain't no need for this,' he said. 'I ain't armed no more.

Listen, I got a hundred Winchesters in that wagon. Fighting Eagle is waiting for 'em five miles east o' here. When he takes Reckless he's gonna take the bank. He's gonna give me all the money. Money ain't no use to him.' The Preacher laughed. 'You kin have half. More money than you can spend. Think of it. You kin head out to California. Any place. Somewhere's where they don't know you. . . .'

John raised his gun.

'I told you what I want.'

The Preacher was nonplussed for a moment. John pulled back the hammer on his gun.

'Sure, sure. You want the watch.' He felt in his waistcoat pocket. 'You kin have it.' He began to unhook the chain from his buttonhole. 'Look, I bin thinkin'. You take all the rifles. Take 'em all. I give 'em to you. Then all the money's yours. All of it.'

The Preacher held out the watch in his left hand, the chain hanging down between his fingers. He flicked open the lid and the sweet chimes sounded in the open prairie. 'This remind you of any place, Yankee boy?' At the same time he went for his Colt, grabbed it and fired, diving to one side as he did so. But John was too quick for him. His shot struck the Preacher in the heart. John walked through the grass, picked up the watch and snapped the lid shut. The only sound was the wind in the high grass. Looking back towards Reckless, John could make out a white dust-cloud and sunlight glinting on the bridles of a column of troopers.

A few minutes later the sound of thunder broke over the plain. Hoofbeats of the troopers' horses shook the ground. John waved them over. The column drew to a halt and the sergeant ordered the men to dismount. He led the men over to the wagon while the lieutenant approached John.

'I was sent out here to arrest you,' the lieutenant said. 'Sure ain't no need for that. Colonel Pride's gonna be impressed with what you've done.'

John showed the lieutenant where the rifles were hidden. The troopers stowed the bodies of the Preacher and his brother in the back among the fruit trees and turned the wagon back towards Reckless.

'I heard you was in Andersonville,' the lieutenant said, as John rode beside him.

John nodded briefly.

'I heard there was terrible things done there.'

'The Preacher did his share of 'em,' John said, and ran his hand over the watch in his pocket.

Colonel Pride had requisitioned a room at the back of the general store as his office. He was studying a map laid out on the table when John knocked on the door. Southern Minnesota, Northern Idaho, their towns, rivers and lakes were all clearly marked, as was the projected route of the new railroad running north from Kansas. But the area on the western side of the map was blank, with just one thin line running east to west out of Fort Trenton. This was the trail the wagons would be following through the Dakota Territories.

The colonel was trying to decide where Fighting Eagle would attack first, the wagon train or the town. He asked himself the question he always asked. If I was the enemy, what would I do?'

The answer was clear to him: the town. The real prize for Fighting Eagle was a military one and this was where the majority of the troopers were. One wagon train more or less was of little consequence. He did not believe there were any

Sioux in the mountains despite what the scout had said: they were a plains people and would not venture away from their usual territory. He would give orders to prepare for an Indian attack.

'Enter,' Pride called.

'You sent for me, sir,' John said.

Colonel Pride smiled at him. 'I have some good news for you, Mr Wright. I have prepared a paper which stated that you pursued and shot the criminal known as the Preacher and recovered the rifles he was intending to sell to the Sioux. The bounty on his head is one thousand dollars. You are a brave man, Mr Wright. As you are a civilian now, I shall overlook the fact that you went against my orders. However, I shall expect you to make it right with Trooper Bean. I hear you pack one helluva punch.'

'Thank you, sir. I saw the Preacher kill my friend in Andersonville just so as he could steal his watch. I had to find him.'

The colonel nodded. 'One or two of my men were in Andersonville, Mr Wright. Clearly, you have eyes sharper than them.'

John produced the watch. 'It was this gave him away, sir.' He flipped open the lid and the colonel smiled at the sound of the chimes then turned back to the map.

'Sir, there's something else,' John said.

Pride looked up.

'Sir, I recovered the money from the bank robbery in Calamity. I hid it, sir, an' I want to hand it back.'

'What regiment were you in, Mr Wright?'

John was surprised by the question. 'First battalion New York Sharpshooters, sir.'

'I knew it,' Pride beamed. 'That regiment has a fine rep-

136

utation. You can always rely on a military man to do the right thing.'

'I ain't no military man,' John said.

'Once a military man, always a military man,' Pride contradicted.

'My home is near Calamity in Wilderness County. I have a family. I must hand the money back. I can't live there if folks regard me as a thief.'

Pride looked John in the eye. 'Quite so. But I'm afraid an escort is out of the question. Fighting Eagle is preparing to attack the town. I can't release any men now, however worthy the cause.' The colonel paused. 'If you have family in Wilderness, you should leave before Fighting Eagle gets here.'

Colonel Pride drew himself up to his full height. 'You can hand the money over to me. I shall write you an official receipt signed by me which you can show to the bank in Calamity. The money will be held at Fort Trenton. The bank can make arrangements to recover it in due course.'

'Thank you, sir. I am obliged,' John said.

'But for now, you need not fear for the safety of the money. I shall lock it away in the bank safe here in Reckless.'

'But, sir—' John began.

'I won't hear another word. I saw that safe myself on my inspection of the town. No one can penetrate those steel doors.' Pride laughed. 'Come back here in an hour. Bring the money and I shall have the paper ready for you.'

Lincoln sawed through the final strip of leather binding his ankles to the tree trunk. He found his Peacemakers in the brush and shoved them back in his holsters, then gestured to Hannah to follow him. They could hear the voices of the braves down by the lake. They trod as quietly as they could through the undergrowth, they found a deer track and followed it up towards the ridge.

Every so often, Lincoln froze and listened. Hannah expected the sound of someone chasing them. She waited for the momentary hiss of an arrow just before it hit. If they were caught, the braves would kill them.

But nothing happened. Each time they paused, expecting to hear footsteps, there was nothing. When they strained to hear voices, it was just the sound of wind in the trees. Lincoln beckoned Hannah on. They were far enough away from the camp now not to worry about making a noise and they started to run. They smashed through thorns and saplings. Branches whipped their faces. The ground was rising steeply now and they pushed on, their hearts hammering, breath clawing their lungs.

On the crest of the ridge, they found the bodies of the troopers whom Pride had sent with Lincoln. All of them had been shot with arrows in the chest and the sides and then the arrows had been torn out of their bodies, to be used again. They lay where they had fallen from their horses. The horses were gone. Lincoln moved from one man to another and felt for a pulse. All the bodies were cold.

Then they heard shouts from below. Some of the Sioux were calling others up from the lake. The braves were searching for them in the undergrowth.

'Left my horse near here,' Lincoln said. 'If he ain't been took.'

Lincoln hurtled down the far side of the ridge. Hannah followed. They could hear the shouts of the Sioux behind them, and could see the plain and the trail to Reckless up ahead. Lincoln stopped and dived off into the woods at the side of the path.

'Wait here,' he called.

Hannah tried to catch her breath. Her bare feet were bloody and swollen. Pain, which she had not noticed before, burned through them. Lincoln appeared mounted on his stallion. He reached down, hauled her up behind him and urged the horse on down the track.

When they emerged from the wooded slope on to the plain, Lincoln pressed his heels into the horse's sides. The great beast leapt forward. They galloped with the wind streaming in their faces. The stallion's hoofbeats sounded a drum roll over the prairie as they charged towards Reckless and towards safety.

14

Safety was in sight. The rooftops of Reckless were a mile ahead. Lincoln drew in the reins and slowed his horse. He looked back over his shoulder. No one was following. He leaned forward and patted the stallion's neck and whispered praise and thanks in his ear.

'Why ain't they coming after us?' Hannah said, still holding on to Lincoln's waist.

'Don't want to show themselves, I guess,' Lincoln said. 'Maybe they're hoping the colonel will send more troopers.'

'To look for the ones he already sent?'

'I warned the colonel about this,' Lincoln said. 'He still thinks because he's got more rifles, Fighting Eagle is gonna be scared of him. He ain't. The colonel thinks like a white man, an' a cavalry officer at that. If Fighting Eagle had more rifles, the colonel knows he an' all the other troopers would be runnin' scared, but that don't mean it's gotta work the other way round.'

Hannah smiled. 'Fighting Eagle ain't afraid of no one. Rifles or none.'

'Fighting Eagle has made the colonel divide the regiment. He sent a detachment to look for me. They're all dead. Then he's gonna leave troopers in Reckless and send some out with the wagons. Those braves up at Paradise Lake, the ones who jumped us, will be riding back to join Fighting Eagle right now. Then all his warriors will be together.'

The prairie ahead of them seemed to stretch to the edge of the world. Green and silver buffalo grass surged and eddied as currents of warm breeze flowed through it. The blue sky arched over the plain, marked only by faint cirrus clouds above the horizon. The golden sun shone. A line of smoke rose over Reckless as if someone had lit a cooking fire.

Lincoln checked again to see that they were not being followed and urged his horse into a trot. He and Hannah watched the line of smoke grow darker until it hung in the bright morning like the pall from a funeral pyre. Then a rider appeared in the distance, circling wide around the town from the west. He changed direction slightly as they watched and headed straight for them at a gallop. Lincoln reined in the stallion again. They stood and waited. It was a trooper, riding hard. He was leaning to one side in his saddle.

When the rider reached them, Lincoln recognized one of Colonel Pride's lieutenants. There was a Sioux arrow buried deep in his left shoulder. Loss of blood had bleached his face. He gripped the reins in his right hand. His left arm hung uselessly at his side. He leaned forward in his saddle.

'We didn't have a chance,' he said. His eyes pleaded with them. 'There was so many of 'em. They just kept comin' and comin'. They went for the troopers first. They'd planned it all. Then they started in on the wagons.'

141

'The wagons?' Lincoln said. 'Ain't you come from Reckless?'

'Colonel sent me with a detachment to accompany the wagons west to Fort Trenton.' The lieutenant paused. 'There was women and children in them wagons.'

'There was men with guns too,' Lincoln said. 'You expect Fighting Eagle to worry about a few women and children?'

'Damn savages,' the lieutenant spat. Then he seemed to see Hannah for the first time. 'You got yourself a Sioux squaw, Scout?'

Hannah looked away, avoiding the lieutenant's eye. She let Lincoln answer.

'Don't waste your breath,' Lincoln said. 'You think they wouldn't kill her just as quick as they'd kill you or me? Anyhow, we thought Reckless was burnin'.'

'That's the train, two miles west. Looks like it's Reckless from here,' the lieutenant said. 'Some braves was followin' me. I didn't want to ride direct to the town so I circled round.'

'Wouldn't have made no difference,' Lincoln said. 'They would've doubled back anyways. How come they surprised you? Didn't you have no one ridin' point?'

'No. Land looked flat. Looked like we could see for miles. But there was a rise in it. Fighting Eagle was the other side of that waitin' for us. He guessed which way we were comin'. We didn't have a chance. They were on us in a minute.'

'We better get back to Reckless before the Sioux get there,' Lincoln said. 'They're gonna need all the help they kin get. You're gonna need to get that shoulder seen to.'

The lieutenant paused. 'I ain't comin'.'

'What?'

'I got another mission. I aim to cross the mountain an' inform Calamity of what's happened here. That will give folks there a chance to prepare for an attack.'

'Whose orders are you actin' on?'

'That ain't your business, Scout. The people of Calamity have got to be informed.'

Lincoln was silent for a minute.

'You're desertin', ain't you?'

The lieutenant was already wheeling his horse around. He jabbed his spurs into the horse's flank.

'Reckless ain't got a chance,' the lieutenant called, as he rode off. 'There's too many of 'em.'

'There's braves in the mountains,' Lincoln hollered. 'They'll kill you before you see 'em.'

'That's a lie, Scout,' the lieutenant shouted back. 'Sioux never go into the mountains.'

The lieutenant urged his horse on and rode away from them.

Lincoln clicked his tongue and his stallion headed towards Reckless again. He turned to speak to Hannah.

'Those braves will have seen the smoke from the wagon train and will be comin' down from the mountain. The lieutenant's gonna run right into 'em.'

Hannah did not answer.

They rode right into Main Street. The troopers and the townsmen were on the rooftops again, but with the wagon train out of town, there were only a few carts left to blockade the alleys. They heard the sergeant's order to the men to hold their fire. As Lincoln and Hannah dismounted, Colonel Pride walked towards them. He touched his hat in a brisk salute and nodded to Lincoln.

'News?'

Lincoln told him about the search party he had sent to look for them and he told him about the lieutenant running from the wagon train. Colour drained from the colonel's face.

'Lieutenant Carson?' he repeated. 'Run off to Calamity? That's desertion. The man will hang for it.'

'Sir—' Lincoln began.

'What is it?'

'We haven't much time, sir. I suggest we attack now. Fighting Eagle won't be expecting—'

'Attack? We have lost over a third of our men.'

'Sir,' Lincoln persisted, 'Fighting Eagle won't be expecting this. We'd catch him off guard.'

Colonel Pride seemed to see Lincoln clearly for the first time.

'If we take the fight to him an' he can see we ain't beat, he might head back to the reservation to regroup. That'll give us time to call for reinforcements and it will save the town.'

Colonel Pride said, 'We ain't got enough men to leave anyone to protect the town.'

'That's right, Colonel,' Lincoln agreed. 'The town will have to protect itself.'

'One good piece of news is that we caught a gunrunner before he had the chance to pass on the rifles to Fighting Eagle. Fighting Eagle has a handful of Winchesters, that's all. We have superior fire power. You're right, Scout, we should take advantage of it.'

Colonel Pride called the sergeant and gave the order for the troopers to be mounted and ready to head out in fifteen minutes. He turned back to Lincoln.

'Who is this woman?'

'She rescued me from the Sioux braves near Lake Paradise, sir,' Lincoln said. 'She's looking for a man named John Wright. She's travelled here alone from Calamity.'

'Wright is a brave and honourable man.'

'He's here?' Hannah burst out.

'He apprehended the gunrunners, ma'am. He got to them ahead of the troopers. I signed the verification for the bounty myself. He also recovered the proceeds of a robbery. I should be surprised if that doesn't carry a reward too.'

The troopers fell in and the sergeant called them to attention. They stood proud in their uniforms, the harnesses of their mounts jingling while Colonel Pride addressed them. With the sun at his back, he seemed to his men to be wearing a halo of fire. He reminded them of their reputation for bravery. He told them that decisive action leads to victory. He told them that with their superior weapons they would win every fight. He told them that their cause was right. There was such passion in the colonel's voice that the men cheered him. The colonel acknowledged their esteem with a wave of his hand. He mounted up and took his place at the head of the column.

Hannah stood on the far side of the dusty street. She listened to the colonel's ringing words and watched the column of troopers ride out. Lincoln was riding point. As the column moved out, a man was left standing opposite her. It was John. He and Hannah ran towards each other, threw their arms around each other and clasped one another tight.

John held her at arm's length so he could look into her eyes. Then he said, 'What the hell are you doin' here?' They both laughed at the banality of the words.

'I heard you were in trouble,' Hannah said. 'I had to

come. Did a dog bite your ear?'

'Yeah. A helluva dog.'

'In the store, they said there had been a robbery. Lincoln recognized you. He rode out and told me.'

'I know, Mikey tricked me,' John said. 'What about William?'

'He's staying with Mr Morgan at the store. He'll be OK. I came because I thought you were in danger.' A shadow of worry crossed Hannah's face. 'The colonel told me about the bounty.'

'I got the letters of verification right here.' John patted his pocket. 'I have to take them to the bank at Calamity. And yourself,' John said. 'You're well?'

Hannah took his hand and placed it on her belly. She smiled at him.

'Are you gonna stay here and fight with the colonel?' she asked.

'Hell, no.' John grinned. 'I'm ridin' home with you. This war with Fighting Eagle is crazy. There ain't gonna be no winners. The colonel will push the Sioux back to the reservation. Troopers will be killed. Braves will be killed. Then, in a few months, Fighting Eagle will attack again. Just because he's back on the reservation don't mean he wants to stay there. This is his land he's fighting for.'

'We ridin' out tonight?' Hannah said.

'Soon as we can. Safest if we go while the troopers are keeping Fighting Eagle busy. Once we're past Pearl there won't be no trouble.'

15

John and Hannah stood by the polished oak desk in the Wells Fargo Bank office in Calamity, waiting for the manager, Samuel Shoddy, to finish reading. Shoddy pushed his spectacles up on to his forehead and held Colonel Pride's letter up to the light from the window. He read it twice then placed it carefully on the desk in front of him.

Shoddy had run the branch since it opened ten years ago. Calamity was a small place. He knew all its inhabitants and most of the folks from the outlying farms. He had never met these two before, but he had heard about their poor dirt farm at the forest edge. Local gossip said the woman had thrown her husband out and taken up with a man half his age. Added to that, the woman was Sioux. And there she was standing in his office as bold as brass.

Shoddy gave a professional beam. 'This is clearly a genuine letter, Mr Wright. You are to be congratulated on saving the bank's money. I shall contact Kansas right away. There is sure to be a reward for this.'

The manager didn't know what to think. A letter bearing Colonel Pride's signature was an important document. The man had recovered a significant sum of money which would show up well in his branch's monthly returns to the Kansas office. Yet the two of them stood there like a couple of saddle tramps, covered in trail dust. And, curiously, the Indian woman was barefoot and seemed to be dressed in man's clothes.

John handed Shoddy a second letter.

'Another. . . .' began Shoddy and held it up to the light from the window. He read the letter twice. John and Hannah waited for him to finish.

'I shall be in touch with the Kansas office. This bounty is payable by the government through the bank.' He ventured a joke. 'Any more letters, Mr Wright?'

'That's all,' John said.

'Well now' – Shoddy stood up from behind his desk – 'I'll send a rider out when we have verification of the funds from the Kansas office. A small branch like this isn't authorized to hand over reward money without verification. Shouldn't take more 'n a week or two.' Shoddy smiled cheerfully. He looked past Hannah, directly at John. 'There won't be any need for you both to come in to collect the money. I'll only be requirin' your signature, Mr Wright, just to confirm you're in receipt of the reward.'

Shoddy leaned across the desk and shook John's hand. 'I'd like to offer you my personal congratulations. There ain't many would've handed in the bank's money if they came across it after a robbery.'

'We try to be decent people,' John said. 'Wilderness County is our home.'

On the way out of town, Hannah saw Mr Morgan standing in the doorway of his store. He waved them over.

'I ain't seen William for days,' he said. 'He stayed here for two nights. Then he took off one morning and I ain't seen him since. Got fed up with Mrs Morgan fussing over him, I guess. He'd rather be out in the woods with that hunting rifle of his.'

Hannah thanked him for his concern. John noticed an anxious look in her eyes.

The trail from Calamity to the farm was over land beaten hard by the summer heat. The topsoil had been dried to dust by the sun and snatched away by the wind. The prairie grass was thin and dry. There were no trees. Only low thorn bushes grew strong. Now, in early autumn, the air was colder. In a few weeks, there would be snow.

When the cabin came in to view, Hannah was surprised not to see smoke coming from the chimney. She had imagined William there waiting to welcome her. She dismounted quickly and ran inside, calling his name, suddenly desperate to see him.

'He's probably out in the woods somewhere,' John said.

John found that the stable had not been swept. Piles of hay were collapsing on to the floor. The hayfork hung in its place on the back of the stable door. John kicked the pile of straw. It had not been turned for days. Looking around the barn, John realized that the place had not been tidied since he had been away.

In the yard, John's annoyance turned to anger. William hadn't let the chickens out. Their water dishes were empty. He stooped down to unlatch the hutch door. The birds tumbled out into the fresh air squawking with relief. John gagged at the stink from inside the hutch. He lifted it off the ground. There were eggs uncollected in the laying boxes. A dead bird lay, with its eyes missing, where the others had pecked at it. John picked it up and flung it down beside the barn.

Walking over to the house, he saw that the goat was still in its pen. It should be tethered out where there was still some grass. Its water dish was dry. William, John thought. He had taught him how to look after everything and all he wanted to do was to take the rifle and go out shooting birds. John hauled a bucket up from the well and filled the goat's and the chickens' drinking bowls. He put the bucket down and waited a moment before entering the cabin. He would have to be careful of what he said. Hannah hated him to be displeased with William.

Inside the cabin, Hannah was sitting on the floor. The room looked as if a twister had passed through it. The table and chairs were overturned. One of the beds was on its side. Blankets, clothes and cooking pots were strewn everywhere. The log pile was spilled across the floor and ash had been raked out from the fire. In places, it even looked as though someone had tried to lever up the floorboards.

Hannah looked up at John. She pointed to a dark stain on the floor.

'It's blood, ain't it?' she said.

'I guess.'

John saw that the hunting rifle was missing from its usual place by the door.

'I told William to go to Mr Morgan at the store if there was trouble,' Hannah said.

'I could ride up through the woods,' John said. 'Where else is there for 'im to go?'

'You could search the woods all day and not find nothin'. All you can do is stand at the edge of the north pasture and holler.' Hannah said. 'If we light a fire, he'll know we're home. You can see the smoke for miles. That's what I'm gonna do.'

Hannah stood up, found the brush and began to sweep the grate.

'You notice anything missing?' she said.

'The hunting rifle. But William would've taken that with him everywhere he went. The goats hadn't been let out. Or the chickens.'

Hannah nodded and started to build a pile of kindling in the grate.

John went outside. He freed the goat from his pen and tethered him to his usual post. The chickens clucked and pecked in the dust. He looked for tracks, but he could only make out the hoofprints of his own horse. He walked round behind the cabin, but there was nothing amiss.

The grass was trodden down on the path to the woods through the north pasture, but no more than usual. John scanned the line of trees, but saw no one. He walked up to the edge of the woods and shouted William's name. There was no answer. John strained to hear, but there was nothing except for the wind in the high branches. Hannah was right. It was best to make a fire and wait.

By the time evening approached, John had swept in front of the house, fed the goat and the chickens and turned the hay in the barn. He found that a leg of one of the old chairs on the porch was broken. He nailed it and bound it tight with twine. The fire was burning and Hannah had put beans on to boil. She had lit the oil lamp and placed it in the centre of the table opposite the window. She started cleaning the cooking pots to keep herself busy.

Darkness fell. Hannah served up soup and they ate in front of the fire. She watched John buckle on his gunbelt but said nothing. John could see the lines of worry etched in her face.

'He's strong,' John said. 'He'll be all right.'

Hannah smiled at him. She moved her chair next to the fire and stared into the flames.

'You intendin' on readin' a little?' John asked. 'When you read them stories to William, I hear 'em too.'

'I can't find the Bible,' Hannah said. 'I left it right here on the mantelshelf. I told William he had to practise his readin' every day. He said he would.'

John moved his chair opposite Hannah's beside the grate. He watched the flames curl and dance. Shapes and faces appeared and disappeared, angels and demons, horror and delight.

'I should've made some coffee,' Hannah said. 'I forgot.' She stood up. 'I'll have to fetch some water from the well. None left in here.' She picked up the pail and walked towards the door.

'Want me to go?' John said.

'No, I'll do it.'

She opened the door and the flames leapt out from the fireplace and roared in the chimney. While she was gone, John drew his Colt and spun the chamber, checking that it was loaded. He pushed it back into his holster and went back to staring at the fire. As Hannah came in again, the flames danced out of the grate.

'Wind's gettin' up,' she said.

There was a crack, like a branch breaking. John and Hannah looked towards the window. A pistol shot. Then there was another. The lamp exploded. Glass and burning oil sprayed across the wooden table. Hannah screamed. John snatched his gun out of its holster, pulled Hannah to the floor and threw himself over her. They lay there for a second and then they could make out a man's laughter above the sound of the wind.

'That was a helluva shot,' the man shouted. 'You best put that fire out or the whole cabin'll be burning.'

'Mikey?' John called.

'I got someone out here who's anxious to see you,' Mikey shouted. 'I'm minded to put a bullet in his head right now unless I get what I want. I only kept 'im alive till I could see you.'

'William,' Hannah gasped. She looked at John.

John stood up, keeping out of the line of the window. Burning oil spread across the table and dripped on to the floor.

'I don't believe you've got anyone out there,' John shouted.

Mikey's laugh sounded harsh and mocking. 'Wanna hear 'im squeal?'

Then it was William's voice, half choking, half a scream.

'Don' give 'im nothin', Pa. Shoot 'im, Pa.' Then he said something else, but his words were wrenched away.

Hannah gripped John's arm.

'I ain't in the mood for talkin' no more.' It was Mikey again. 'You know what I come fer.'

'You let 'im go. You can have me instead,' John shouted. 'I'm throwin' out my gun.'

John threw his Colt out of the window.

'See that? I ain't armed.'

'An' the Winchester,' Mikey called. 'An' the shotgun.'

'I'm comin out,' he yelled. 'We ain't got the Winchester nor the shotgun no more. Indians took 'em.'

John opened the door. The fire roared in the grate. Outside, the high branches beat against the wind. Mikey was standing close to the window, at the side of the cabin.

His Colt was pointed at William, who was kneeling on the ground beside him. A noose was around William's neck and his hands were tied behind his back. Mikey gripped the noose tight. Their faces were lit by the firelight through the window.

'You left me for dead,' Mikey said. His voice was steel. 'An' you stole my money. There ain't no reason why I shouldn't shoot you, this kid an' the squaw right now.'

'Let 'im go,' John said. 'Then we'll talk.'

Mikey jerked the noose tighter. William turned his face upwards to try to snatch a breath. In the flickering light, John saw that the boy's face was masked with bruises. 'I ain't got nothing to say to you. You just hand over the money from the Calamity Bank. That's what you're gonna do right now.'

'I ain't got it,' John said.

The cabin door opened. Hannah stood there with the firelight dancing behind her.

'What d'ya mean? Where is it?' Mikey cocked his gun.

'I handed it in,' John said.

'I'm gonna spread the kid's brains right across that wall unless you give me the money.' He yanked the noose again and pressed the barrel of his gun up against William's temple.

'He's tellin the truth,' Hannah said.

Mikey threw down the noose and kicked William aside. He pointed the gun at Hannah. John knelt and loosened the rope and William gulped in air, coughing and choking. John cut the rope which tied the boy's hands and pulled him towards the cabin away from Mikey. Then he stood up.

'You're tellin' me you gave the money back to the bank?' Mikey said. He was bewildered. 'When they didn't even know it was you that took it in the first place?' He looked from Hannah to John. 'Is that what you're tellin' me? An' they gave you a reward, is that it? You kin give me the reward money then.'

'They ain't said nothing about a reward.'

'You're a lyin' sonofabitch. You left me for dead. I woke up expectin' to see you there. But you was gone. There wasn't no one there. I crawled away into the bushes an' hid myself good. Damn fool posse couldn't find me.' Mikey laughed. 'An Irish boy from Five Points is more 'n a match for any damn deputy. More 'n a match fer you. I headed straight back up here. Your boy looked after me for a coupla days. Then he started to want to go into town. He told some story about he was supposed to be livin' at the store, so I had to keep 'im on a leash like a dog to stop 'im from running off.' Mikey laughed again.

John could see a dark bloodstain seeping through Mikey's shirt. His gun wavered.

'Take me with you,' Hannah said. 'Leave them. I'll go with you.'

Mikey levelled his gun at her.

'What would I want with an Injun squaw?' he sneered.

In a second, William made a dive for the Winchester in the shadows below the window. Mikey swung his gun round. John launched himself at him. A shot ricocheted off the cabin wall. John was wrestling Mikey's gun away from him. William found the Winchester and stood over the men.

'No,' Hannah screamed.

William hesitated.

The men wrestled hard. Then John pinned Mikey's hand holding the gun on the ground. He brought his other arm back and socked Mikey on the jaw with a right like a hammer. Mikey's body relaxed for a second as the force of the blow juddered through him. He dropped the .45. Then he gathered his strength and shoved John away.

John dived for the gun. They pulled at it between them. Each man summoned all his strength. They rolled in the shadows on the hard ground, each trying to twist the aim of the gun towards the other. There was a shot. The wind roared in the trees. The men rolled apart. Hannah and William drew back against the cabin wall, unable to see what had happened.

John staggered to his feet, clutching his left hand, crying out in pain. He kicked the gun aside. Mikey lay still. Hannah ran to John and held him for a moment, then drew him towards the door.

Inside the cabin, Hannah guided John towards the bed and examined his smashed hand. 'Had my hand over the barrel. Forced it round on 'im,' John said. 'When he fired, bullet went through my hand an' killed 'im stone dead.'

Hannah found the whiskey bottle and poured John a slug. Then she splashed it over his hand. Fine white bones were sticking out through the skin.

'William, you can ride into town as soon as it's light and fetch the doctor. I ain't even gonna bandage this.'

She placed his hand on a cotton pad made from a torn-up shirt and covered it lightly.

William put the two handguns down on the table. He drew in his breath at the sight of John's hand.

John said, 'Any of that whiskey left?' He smiled at William through the pain. 'You did good. Now, let your mother see to your face.'

EPILOGUE

Six Weeks Later

William saw the lone rider first. He ran into the cabin, bursting with excitement. 'He's comin', Ma.'

Hannah brushed the flour off her hands and left the pile of sourdough on the table. John got up out of his chair and the three of them went out on to the porch to see.

The man rode out of the hard land against a steel sky. The first snow had already come and gone. The farm was prepared for winter. The reward money had enabled John and Hannah to lay in more supplies than they had ever had before. They had bought a horse from a dealer who passed through Calamity and the grain field was ploughed, ready for spring. John had bought in extra hay and the barn was almost full.

William had done most of the ploughing as John's arm was still in a sling. The doctor had showed Hannah how to bind John's hand in a splint and told her when to renew the dressings. But his left hand would always be useless now.

Lincoln had come to take William off to join the regiment. Fighting Eagle was back on the reservation which meant he would stay there for the winter. Colonel Pride and his troopers had been ordered south into Kansas, where there had been trouble with the Pawnee earlier in the year. Lincoln was going to take William with him.

'I ain't callin' him Pa. I'll call him by his name,' William said, as they watched the rider approach.

'I think he'll like that,' Hannah said. 'You got everythin'?'

William went to fetch his horse from the barn as Lincoln rode up to the house. Lincoln nodded a greeting to them.

'I got coffee on the stove,' Hannah said.

'I ain't stayin',' Lincoln said. 'But I'd thank you to bring me a cup out.'

Hannah went into the cabin and Lincoln turned to John.

'How's the hand?'

'Healin',' John said. 'Won't be much use to me in the future though.'

'I'll have the boy back in time to help with the spring plantin'. You don't have to worry 'bout that.'

John shrugged. 'Maybe you'll make a scout of him an' he won't want to come back.'

Lincoln laughed. 'That's his mother talkin'. He'll always want to come back. This is his home.'

'You didn't,' John said.

'I was raised on the frontier. That's what I know best. I just want to show William what it's like before it all disappears. It'll all be gone way before he's grown old. There'll be governed states from here to California, an' railroads every which way. You see if I ain't right.'

Hannah came out of the cabin and handed Lincoln a tin mug of coffee.

'Anyhow,' Lincoln went on, 'I hear you got reward

money for the fella that robbed the Calamity bank as well as that gunrunner in Reckless. Your reputation sure is ace high in Wilderness.'

Hannah stood beside John on the porch. William led his horse out of the barn and mounted up.

'Hear that, William?' Hannah said.

'I sure did, Ma.' He grinned proudly at John.

Hannah linked her arm in John's.

'You ready for the frontier, young fella?' Lincoln said.

'Yes I am, Lincoln.'

Lincoln smiled at him.

'You take care now,' John called. 'Both of you.'

William and Lincoln turned their horses south.

'So long, Ma, so long, John,' William called. 'See you in the spring.'

John and Hannah stood on the porch and watched the riders until they were down the trail and out of sight. The sky was grey and heavy with snow, but inside the cabin the fire blazed strong. John rested his hand on Hannah's belly.

'Baby'll be due just about the time William gets home, I reckon,' he said.

Hannah smiled up at him. 'I reckon so.'

They went inside and closed the door. Hannah went back to kneading the pile of sourdough on the table. John took a chair by the fire.

'Think William's got the frontier in him?' John asked.

Hannah put down the dough, thought for a minute. Then she said, 'I reckon we all got the frontier in us somewhere. It's the place where you do what has to be done an' you try to do it right.' She looked across at John. 'That's what you did. That's why we're proud of you.'

John stared at the fire. Horsemen reared out of the

flames; faces and shadows came and went. Hannah went back to her baking. Her dark hair fell across her face as she leaned over the table, pressing and stretching the dough. Eventually, she gathered it and set it to prove in a bowl beside the fire. She swept the remaining flour off the table.

'I'm looking forward to that bread,' John said. 'Ain't nothin' like the smell of bakin' bread in a cabin.'

'Smell o' coffee's pretty nice too,' Hannah said.

John laughed. He looked her in the eye. 'OK. I'll make some fresh. Then you come and sit down here beside me an' we can talk about how we're gonna go about plantin' up the farm in the spring.'